"Do you want children of your own someday?" Jared asked.

"I do," she answered truthfully, but then realized she didn't have to bear an infant to be a mother. She'd be perfectly happy mothering Jared's daughters.

The thought stopped her cold. She hadn't realized she was falling for Jared so completely. Or how his twins had captured her heart.

She'd better not weave fantasies and dreams. He didn't want an involvement. She shouldn't take the risk.

Just then, Jared's pager went off. He checked the number. "It's my mother's surgeon. I'm going to go outside to call."

She watched Jared as he hurried into the anteroom. Dreams of wedding bells and lace with a partner who was tender and passionate and who loved with all his heart could never come true for her. At thirty-two, she was too old to believe in fairy tales.

Wasn't she?

Dear Reader,

I grew up believing in fairy tales. In college, when I met my husband-to-be, I still believed in them. A few Christmases ago he proved he believes, too, by giving me a glass slipper. I don't think a woman needs a castle or jewels to feel like Cinderella. She simply needs a man who will give her his heart, devotion and commitment.

My heroine, Emily Diaz, was starting her life over. She didn't expect a prince to gallop into her world and rescue her. My hero, Dr. Jared Madison, was wounded by his past, and didn't intend to fall in love ever again. Yet he fell in love with Emily. This couple discovered they could heal each other's hearts. Jared was Emily's prince-in-disguise and Emily became Jared's modern-day Cinderella.

I hope you enjoy *The Midwife's Glass Slipper* and believe in fairy tales again.

All my best,

Karen Rose Smith

THE MIDWIFE'S GLASS SLIPPER

KAREN ROSE SMITH

SPECIAL EDITION®

Published by Silhouette Books

America's Publisher of Contemporary Romance

If you purchased this book without a cover you should be aware that this book is stolen property. It was reported as "unsold and destroyed" to the publisher, and neither the author nor the publisher has received any payment for this "stripped book."

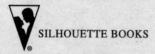

SILHOUETTE BOOKS

ISBN-13: 978-0-373-65454-3
ISBN-10:   0-373-65454-5

Recycling programs
for this product may
not exist in your area.

THE MIDWIFE'S GLASS SLIPPER

Copyright © 2009 by Karen Rose Smith

All rights reserved. Except for use in any review, the reproduction or utilization of this work in whole or in part in any form by any electronic, mechanical or other means, now known or hereafter invented, including xerography, photocopying and recording, or in any information storage or retrieval system, is forbidden without the written permission of the editorial office, Silhouette Books, 233 Broadway, New York, NY 10279 U.S.A.

This is a work of fiction. Names, characters, places and incidents are either the product of the author's imagination or are used fictitiously, and any resemblance to actual persons, living or dead, business establishments, events or locales is entirely coincidental.

This edition published by arrangement with Harlequin Books S.A.

® and TM are trademarks of Harlequin Books S.A., used under license. Trademarks indicated with ® are registered in the United States Patent and Trademark Office, the Canadian Trade Marks Office and in other countries.

Visit Silhouette Books at www.eHarlequin.com

Printed in U.S.A.

KAREN ROSE SMITH

Award-winning and bestselling author Karen Rose Smith has seen more than sixty novels published since 1991. Living in Pennsylvania with her husband—who was her college sweetheart—and their two cats, she has been writing full-time since the start of her career. She enjoys researching and visiting the West and Southwest, where this series of books is set. Readers can receive updates on Karen's latest releases and write to her through her Web site at www.karenrosesmith.com, or at P.O. Box 1545, Hanover, PA 17331.

To my husband Steve—
may we always believe in fairytales.

Chapter One

Rising from the desk in her office, Emily Diaz hurried into the hall at the sound of children's laughter.

Dr. Jared Madison stood there, his shock of dark-brown hair falling over his brow, his tie askew. He held the hands of his identical twin daughters. Usually the epitome of calm and tact, he dropped the stuffed unicorn he'd clutched under one arm.

One of the little girls—both were dressed in Cinderella T-shirts and pink shorts—let go of his hand and warned, "Don't step on Stardust!"

"I'd never do that," the physician replied, his Texas drawl more evident this morning than it usually was. He spotted Emily as his daughter saved the unicorn.

Emily didn't know quite what to say. Dr. Madison had hired her over seven months ago to be his obstetrical nurse practitioner. Ever since she'd interviewed for the position, she'd felt…a current between them, though Dr. Madison had never been anything but professional. She'd told herself more than once that she wouldn't get involved personally because she valued her job and because…

She shivered to think of the consequences for her job if he learned her secret.

"Who are you?" the twin not clutching Stardust piped up. Both girls were adorable with light-brown hair and huge green eyes, the same color green as their father's.

Without thinking, Emily dropped down to the their eye level, her own black, very curly hair flowing forward to tickle her chin. She kept it banded back when she examined patients, but this morning she'd intended to spend a quiet morning in her office catching up on paperwork. "My name is Emily, and I work with your dad."

Everyone knew Dr. Madison had twin, three-year-old daughters, though that was about all they knew. He was a very private man. One very tall, broad-shouldered, *sexy* man.

Emily tried to ignore him as she concentrated on the two little girls. "What are your names?" She glanced up at the physician, hoping he wouldn't mind her asking.

The twins checked with their dad and he gave a nod.

"Amy," the twin on the left easily told Emily.

The little girl on the right poked her finger into her mouth, studied Emily for a few moments, then mumbled, "I'm Courtney."

Amy added, "Daddy's taking care of us because Grandma fell boom."

"Honey, how about if you and Amy go into my office?" He opened the door across the hall and gestured the girls inside.

His daughters ran into the office as if they'd never been

there before, peering at everything in sight—the floor-to-ceiling bookshelves, the long mahogany desk, the two comfortable padded chairs facing it, the old-fashioned car replicas on the credenza, the coffeepot and packet of sandwich cookies on a side table.

"Cookies!" Courtney cried with glee, heading toward them.

But Dr. Madison was quick. "Oh, no. You just had breakfast."

Striding to his desk, he bent to one of the drawers, opened it and took out several sheets of blank paper. Then he reached into the pencil holder on his desk, plucking out two markers.

He pointed to the carpet at the side of the room. "How about if you draw for a couple of minutes while I find some toys in the waiting room?"

He glanced at Emily, still in the hall. After giving his girls the paper and markers, he met her at the door and lowered his voice. "My mother takes care of them and she fell this morning. Unfortunately, they saw it. The ambulance, too. They were upset and I couldn't get hold of my cousin who watches them sometimes. I had no choice but to bring them in."

He checked his watch. "I'm going to have patients to see in about fifteen minutes. I could try to reroute them to the partners—"

"I'll watch the twins."

As he studied Emily, she could hear every one of her heartbeats. She was wearing a cranberry suit this morning. She'd lost weight over the past year and a half because of everything she'd been through, but she still had a well-rounded figure. Usually it was covered by her yellow smock. Now it wasn't. She didn't know why she'd offered to watch his girls. Maybe it was because she missed being around babies and children. She took care of pregnant moms now, but she didn't assist in deliveries. Back in Corpus Christi, in addition to being a midwife, she used to volunteer at the pediatric unit at the hospital. She thought wistfully of her old life—before the lawsuit and her divorce and the move to Sagebrush, Texas. She was lucky, she told herself, to live a short drive from these offices in Lubbock, at the Family Tree Health Center.

"Why would you want to watch them?" he asked.

She shrugged. "Because I like kids and I don't have patients this morning. My first appointment isn't until one. I don't know what you're going to do this afternoon, but I can cover the morning."

Dr. Madison was a good six inches taller than she was. He looked down at her and suddenly smiled. "How do you know they're not hellions on wheels?"

When she peeked around him into his office, her arm brushed his. Her heart practically stopped from the jolt of electric current. Had he felt it, too?

She quickly scanned what the girls were doing. They were drawing.

When Emily met his gaze again, she saw the glint of interest there. "They look more like cherubs than hellions, and from the way they settled down so quickly, I'd say they're well behaved. But I have been known to be wrong. If I am, you can add a bonus to my salary."

He laughed and seemed surprised he did.

Emily knew Dr. Madison was cordial with his patients. But he was usually serious otherwise. She'd gotten the impression that the lines around his eyes hadn't come from laughing, though maybe they'd been deepened by it with his daughters. In his early forties, he was a widower. Emily wondered if his serious nature and the lines on his face had something to do with that.

"I'd be forever grateful if you could handle them for the morning," he decided. "I don't know if there are enough toys in the waiting room to keep them occupied for that long."

"With LEGOs, a miniature farm set to play with and my origami skills, I think we'll be fine."

"Origami skills?" He grinned. "Have you been hiding your talents?"

The word *hiding* made her almost panic. *Calm down!* she told herself. This jumpiness was why she'd never had such a long, personal conversation with Dr. Madison. "Not so hidden. I did a science project on origami when I was in high school. In college, I took to it as an art. So as long as I have paper to fold, the girls might be a little fascinated."

The doctor's cell phone beeped a few times and he snatched it from his belt, opening it. "Excuse me," he said to Emily. "It's Dr. Garcia from the hospital. I asked him to call me as soon as my mother had X-rays."

When he stepped outside the room, Emily stepped inside, but she was still aware of his cologne, still aware of his tall, lean physique, still aware of everything about the man whom she'd admired since he'd hired her.

She sank down to the floor beside the girls. "Tell me about your pictures."

Courtney explained the boxy vehicle she'd drawn had come to their house with lights flashing. Amy's picture, on the other hand, was a stick figure of a man with a stethoscope around his neck. Anyone else examining the picture could have mistaken it for a necklace, but Emily guessed the girls had seen their father wearing it.

When Emily saw Jared had finished his call, she stood and went out to the hall again.

He was frowning, looking troubled. "My mother's hip is broken," he said gruffly. "After discussing it with her, they've decided to do surgery." He sighed and raked his hand through his hair. "That means she'll be in the hospital for a week, rehab for two. I have to get hold of my cousin to see if she'll be willing to help out. She's a free spirit, doesn't like to be tied down, so I don't know how this will play into her plans."

"Dr. Madison, I'm so sorry."

Their gazes met again and Emily felt a shiver of male-female awareness.

"You've been here long enough to call me Jared."

"I didn't think time had anything to do with it. You're my boss."

He gave her a half smile. "I am. But I think those stringent barriers have blurred a bit this morning. Is it all right if I call you Emily?"

She felt her cheeks start to flush. "Yes, that's fine."

"You could take the girls into the lounge," he suggested.

In the very small room with a table and chairs and refrigerator, employees came and went. There wasn't really enough room to gather, even if they had time.

"I think I'll take them to my office. It's bigger. Can they have juice? I know there's some in the refrigerator."

"Juice, but nothing else that's sweet. I'm hoping the morning goes smoothly and I can buy them lunch at the deli."

The Family Tree Health Center really was a center for specialty practices. Conveniently, there was a café on the first floor and a deli cart sandwich station on the second.

"If you get tied up, I'll get them something."

"Emily, do you know what you're volunteering for? Children can be tiring and cranky."

"And an absolute joy. We'll be fine. Really. Trust me."

A shadow passed over Jared's face and Emily wondered whether trust was difficult for him. Why?

Trust wasn't easy for her, either. In fact, except for her housemates, Francesca and Tessa, she usually kept to herself. It had seemed safer, especially in a new place. She had to remind herself Tessa was no longer her housemate. Her friend had gotten married and moved out last week.

"I'll get the toys," Jared said, grounding Emily in the here and now.

His gaze locked with hers again and she seemed mesmerized for a moment by the mysterious green of his eyes. Then he broke the spell and strode toward the reception area.

When Jared's last appointment for the morning canceled, he was almost relieved. He had to see how Emily Diaz and his daughters were faring. He'd looked in on them briefly after their first hour with her, and they hadn't even noticed he was there! Quite a feat, since after they'd lost their mother, they'd stuck to him like glue. It said something about Emily's charm. She'd seemed so…robotic since he'd hired her. Maybe because he'd felt sparks he shouldn't have felt when he'd interviewed her and she'd sensed his masculine interest. Yet, he told himself, there was *no* interest. With a failed marriage that had been mostly his fault, and his daughters to take care of on his own, he wasn't about to get involved with anyone, not even a dark-haired, brown-eyed beauty who might ease his restlessness.

When he peeked into Emily's office, he heard Amy's awe as she said, "It looks like a swan. There's a swan in one of my story books."

"I think I know which one," Emily offered. "*The Ugly Duckling.*"

Both girls nodded vigorously. "What else can you make?" they chorused.

Jared noticed the array of toys on the floor, a daily occurrence at his house, too. The August sun streamed in the window as his twins sat together in one chair beside Emily's desk. She was just around the corner with colored sheets of paper splayed here and there.

When Courtney saw him she scrambled from her chair and hugged him around his legs. "Emily knows how to play with toys. She was a farmer."

"She took the milk to market," Amy piped in.

"Well, you *have* been busy. I happen to have an extra half hour freed up. I brought us lunch." He opened bags on the desk and produced an array of food from sandwiches to salads to fruit cups.

As he settled the girls with a half sandwich each and some milk, he asked Emily, "Would you consider doing this for the afternoon, too?" Unbelievably, he did trust her with his daughters.

"I have patients."

"I know you do. But Tom's OB nurse is free this afternoon and he said he wouldn't mind lending her to me and she's willing to help. I know this is a lot to ask, but I'd really like to keep some continuity with the girls, and I still haven't been able to reach Chloie. Sometimes, when she doesn't want to feel tied down, she'll leave her cell phone at home. So I have no idea where she is."

Jared found himself studying Emily again, wanting to get to know her better. They were across the desk from each other, yet there seemed to be a magnetic pull that shortened the distance between them.

Emily chose a fruit cup from the lunch assortment. "Maybe you'd like to talk to Amy and Courtney and find out if they've been having a good time."

"The smiles on their faces when I came in and their rapt attention to you told me all I need to know."

She looked surprised by the compliment…as if she didn't get many. Then she asked, "If I watch them this afternoon, do you mind if I take them for a walk down to the garden to look at the fountain?"

Jared hesitated.

"I promise I'll hold their hands and never let them out of my sight. I know how precious children are, Jared."

The sound of his name on her lips made his gut tighten. Damn, but he was attracted to her. "All right. But let me know when you leave and when you return."

He'd lost people in his life. He needed to know his daughters were safe.

He instinctively felt they were safe with Emily.

Ever since he'd hired her, something about her had intrigued him. But he'd shut down that intrigue. He'd tried to turn off the current of electricity that vibrated whenever he got close to her. He was the boss. He shouldn't be thinking anything but professional thoughts about her.

At the end of the day, Jared found his daughters with Emily in her office, building houses with glue and tongue depressors.

"Have you gotten hold of your cousin?" she asked as soon as she saw him. She lowered her eyes.

Was she trying to avoid the pull of attraction that he was feeling, too? He'd been away from the dating circuit for so long, maybe he was mistaking her kindness for chemistry.

"I've left messages for her. I'm hoping she'll call me this evening." Then before he even realized what he planned to do, he asked, "Can I repay you tonight with a take-out dinner? Or have you spent enough time in the company of kids?"

He'd never invited a woman back to the house with his girls. Actually, he was hoping for a little adult conversation that wasn't professional in nature. How long had it been since he'd spent a casual evening talking?

Just talking? his conscience asked. He ignored it.

A light pink color rose to Emily's cheeks as her gaze met his again. "I'd like that. But I should go home and change first."

"There's nothing wrong with what you're wearing."

Her eyes widened in surprise as if she hadn't expected him to notice. Oh, he'd noticed all right. Her slim jacket delineated her breasts and molded to her waist. The tailored slacks fit her hips perfectly.

"I thought casual might be better with the girls." Then she blushed. "I don't even know where you live. Do you have a place here in Lubbock?"

"I don't live far from the hospital. You live in Sagebrush, don't you?"

"Yes. I share a house with two friends. Actually one now. Tessa got married last week."

"Tessa McGuire? The pediatrician?"

"Yes. It's Rossi now. Do you know her?"

"We've consulted a few times."

"My other roommate is Francesca Talbot."

He nodded. "The neonatologist. I've consulted with her more than with Dr....Rossi."

"I met them after I took my job here. It's more economical to share a house than—" Her cheeks grew a little pinker. "More information than you need to know," she said with a small smile.

He found he wanted to know so much more about Emily, and that was dangerous. He never intended to marry again. And to get involved when he had little spare time seemed foolish. Yet she was so pretty with her curly hair, high cheekbones and big brown eyes. She had a great figure, too. His ex-wife had always been way too thin. Had the cancer started before anyone knew it? He should have looked closer…deeper.

Courtney took Emily's hand. "Come home wif us?"

She hesitated as if she might be having second thoughts, then smiled. "It *would* be silly of me to drive back to Sagebrush to change. I'll follow you if that's okay."

"Sounds good," Jared agreed, determined to forget about the past at least for tonight and not think too seriously about kissing Emily. It was a good thing his daughters would be around as pint-sized chaperones. He really didn't need an entanglement or a complication in his life, especially now with his mother in the hospital. He'd call her on the way home. He should stop in tonight…. There were never enough hours in the day.

A half hour later, Jared set the takeout on his dining-room table. Emily was at his elbow, close enough to touch. He found the idea of touching her aroused him. His sexual urges had been in deep freeze for so long that he welcomed feeling alive again.

So much for pint-sized chaperones. They were already digging into their toy box in the great room.

"Girls, go on to the bathroom and wash your hands. I'll be there in a minute."

Jared went to the kitchen and Emily followed. "What can I do?"

Apparently she was a doer like he was. "Set the table?" he suggested, opening the cabinet that held dishes.

There were two sets—plain white ironstone dishes and then a collection of cream china with tiny blue roses.

"Oh, how pretty," Emily commented.

"Those are my mother's. She insists we use them every holiday. They have to be hand-washed."

"You don't like the tradition?"

"I never thought of it that way—as a tradition, I mean. When I was growing up—" He stopped short. "Traditions are okay as long as they bring along happy memories with them. Those dishes don't."

Emily looked puzzled, but he wasn't going to go into his background. Not now. Probably not ever.

"I understand you're a widower," Emily said. "How long has it been since your wife died?"

He stopped for a moment, startled because she'd been so direct.

"I'm sorry. Maybe I shouldn't have mentioned it. It's one of the pieces of information everyone at Family Tree has about you."

"*One* of the pieces?" He lifted dishes from the cupboard, not knowing whether to be amused or annoyed.

He could see Emily was flustered, but she went ahead anyway. "Everyone seems to know you're a widower and have three-year-old twin girls."

"Three and a half," he amended. "And if that's all 'everyone' knows, I guess I should consider myself lucky."

After setting the dinnerware on the counter, he leaned back against it and crossed his arms over his chest. As soon as he did it, he knew it was a defensive gesture. He was feeling defensive. Still, Emily's honesty prompted the same kind of honesty from him.

"Two years ago I was divorced. Six months later my wife died of cancer."

"I'm so sorry."

He uncrossed his arms and let them drop to his sides. "Valerie had had custody of the girls and I had liberal visitation rights. But taking over their full care was a real shocker."

"I imagine it must have been."

Usually he didn't want to talk about this with anyone, but he found discussing the situation with Emily wasn't so bad. "My mother stepped in to help. Honestly, I don't know what I would have done without her. Hired a nanny, I guess. That's what I'm going to have to do now until she's back on her feet. I set up an interview with someone from a service tomorrow afternoon."

That was certainly enough about him. He wanted to know more about Emily. "I remember from your application that you were from Corpus Christi."

"Yes, I was born and raised there. I'd never lived anywhere else until I moved to Sagebrush."

"Culture shock?"

"From east Texas to west Texas, beach to plains. I'm getting used to it. I'm even beginning to like it."

"You intend to stay here?"

"I hope to. I like my work. I've made great friends. What else could a girl ask for?"

There was something in Emily's eyes that told him she might like a lot more, children maybe, a family. He noticed she didn't wear perfume, not the kind other women wore, anyway. But she always smelled like a summer garden. Maybe it was her shampoo. Maybe something she dabbed in intimate places.

They were standing close, close enough that if he leaned forward just a little—

But she suddenly caught her breath. He leaned away. Then he cleared his throat and, feeling as awkward as a teenager, mumbled, "I'd better see what trouble the girls are getting into." If that wasn't an exit line, he didn't know what was.

When he and Amy and Courtney returned to the dining room, he stopped short. Emily hadn't just put food on the dishes; she'd set places, napkins included. She'd found a place mat from somewhere, put that in the middle and piled the entrees on platters and the sides in serving dishes. Instead of the plastic forks and spoons from the restaurant, she'd used real silverware.

"I hope you girls are hungry." She pulled out a chair for each of them so they could hop on. She pushed Amy in while he helped Courtney.

Leaning close to him, she said in a low voice, "I thought the girls would have trouble eating with the plastic forks."

"Are you used to spending time with children?" She seemed to know exactly what to do.

"I've never had any of my own, but when I was in Corpus Christi, I volunteered in a pediatric ward when I had time off."

So that's how she'd spent her free time. He was seeing facets of Emily he'd never had time to explore.

"Have you ever been married?" he asked as he pulled her chair out for her.

She looked surprised he'd done the gentlemanly thing. It had been a long time since he'd *wanted* to do the gentlemanly thing.

"Yes, I was married. I've been divorced about a year."

Now it was his turn to ask a blunt question. "Is that why you moved here?"

This time she didn't hesitate. "I needed a fresh start."

His hands were on the chair back, close to her hair. She was looking up at him over her shoulder. He was so tempted to push her curls away from her face, to erase the little frown line on her forehead, to tell her he understood about wanting a new beginning.

Yet he'd figured out the past dogged him no matter where he went, or how badly he tried to forget. Did her past dog her, too?

The urge to ask her was strong and on the tip of his tongue when the cell phone on his belt beeped. He almost swore, and then he realized he should be glad for the inter-ruption. This evening was becoming intense and personal.

Straightening, he unhitched the phone, checked the number and held it to his ear. It was his service. Crossing to the counter, he found a notepad and a pen and jotted down the number.

He said to Emily, "I think Lubbock is about to have a new citizen who doesn't want to wait until its due date. I have to check with the mother-to-be. Go ahead and start eating."

As he dialed his patient, he noticed Emily asking the girls what they wanted and then selecting their food for them and helping them with it. She was so conscious of what they needed…such a natural with them.

When he finished on the phone, she took one look at his face and asked, "Do you need me to stay with the girls?"

He didn't want to ask her to do that. He certainly didn't want to depend on her. If he examined his reasons, they were simple. Today he'd felt a connection with her—a connection that was getting stronger each minute he was with her.

Seeing that the girls were occupied with eating, she pushed back her chair and came over to stand by him. "It's really all right if you need me to stay. I don't have any other commitments."

"I don't know how long this will go. The contractions are three and a half minutes apart, but this is her first baby. Anything can happen."

"Tomorrow's my day off. If you're not back until late, I'll just fall asleep on the couch."

If he was late and if she fell asleep on his couch, some-thing could happen that would startle her awake very fast.

He lowered his voice. "Have you ever heard of night terrors?"

She studied him. "They're a type of children's nightmare."

"Yes, in a way. Though the child often doesn't remember the nightmare after he or she wakes up. Courtney has them. I can't let you stay without warning you about them. And if you don't want to deal with that, I'll have to find another doctor to cover for me."

He fully expected her to be put off by the idea, to want to pick up her purse and leave. Instead, she said, "Explain to me what to do if Courtney has one. As long as I'm prepared, I can handle the situation."

Jared was starting to realize that he'd examined Emily's résumé, phoned her brief reference list and hired her, but he didn't really know her.

Tonight, that could change. He wasn't sure whether he should get to know Emily better…or not.

Chapter Two

Opening her eyes, Emily heard her name as if from a great distance.

"Emily, it's midnight."

The feel of Jared's hand on her shoulder sent tingles throughout her body that brought her awake quickly.

Crouched down beside her, he wore scrubs and smelled as if he'd freshly showered. In fact, his hair was still damp. His muscled arm lay next to hers, almost touching it. His thigh muscles were obvious against the blue cotton fabric. Most of all, she noticed his eyes. They were so green, lighter at first, then more intense, more filled with—

Desire? She hadn't seen desire in a man's eyes for a very long time.

As he leaned closer, her anticipation was as rich as the hunger and need in his eyes. But then he stood and ran his hand over his brow.

She sat up but she didn't want to get her purse and say good-night. She wanted to know if she was right about the vibrations between them.

She patted the sofa next to her. "You look beat. Decompress a little. Tell me about the birth."

When he gazed at her, his eyes were filled with something she didn't understand. Questions. What would he be questioning?

"You really want to hear?"

"Sure! Babies are our business. What's most important to my pregnant moms is what kind of delivery they'll have and if their baby will be healthy. I like to hear what happens after they leave my care."

"I never thought of it that way. You don't usually see the finished result."

An ache enfolded her heart. She *so* missed seeing the finished result. "I go to the hospital nursery and take a peek. Sometimes the moms bring babies back to the office to visit after they're born. But for the most part, I *don't* know what happens after they leave me."

"Tonight was a breeze for a first baby. Leanne's contractions were two and a half minutes apart when I got there. Her husband was a great coach and she had good focus. By eleven thirty, she had a baby girl, and I was ready for a shower."

"What do you feel when it happens?"

He appeared startled for a moment and then gave her a long assessing look. "No one has ever asked me that."

She could see that was true and she wondered why. After all, that feeling was the reason she had delivered baby after baby as a midwife. That feeling was what made it all worthwhile.

He glanced down at his hands as if he was trying to relive the birth. The fatigue left his face. "It's an unexplainable moment. It's a moment when something you believe can't possibly happen, does. It's a moment when life is precious and men understand why they live and fight and die for what they hold dear."

"It's a moment," she murmured, "when heaven meets earth."

He studied her and she realized she'd said too much. She should tell him she knew firsthand all about that moment. Yet because of the lawsuit, he might not want her practicing with him. If she told him her history, this closeness she was feeling to him right now could simply vanish.

"You sound as if you know."

"I've attended births." She didn't add that she was the one who had caught the baby in her hands.

His shoulder brushed hers as he admitted, "In that moment when a child is born, I forget the long hours and the hassles and the schedule shuffling. I guess most of life is that way. We work for the payoff, and if the payoff keeps us satisfied, we keep doing it."

"It's more than a payoff." She remembered the feel of that little wet body in her hands…the eyes coming open…the first cry. How she missed it. How she wished she had the courage to go back and be part of delivering babies all over again.

Jared angled toward her. They were close enough to feel each other's breath. "You really do understand."

"I take care of moms and teach them how to take care of themselves for a reason."

His large hand was so gentle as he stroked her cheek and pushed her curls away from her face. "I've never met anyone like you, Emily. Not everyone can understand the joy of holding a baby. You make what you do and what I do sound like more than a profession. You make it sound special and worthwhile."

"It is." She wanted to say more…she wanted to tell him that's why she'd gone into women's homes to help them have their babies there. She yearned to say that she'd believed in home births because light and love and friendship could surround the newborn before, during and after the moment of birth. Yet she'd come to doubt that ideal. She'd come to doubt her judgment and skill. With those doubts lurking, she could never do it again. She'd be more prone to making a mistake. Mistakes were unacceptable when you were bringing a child into the world.

"What's wrong?" he asked.

She tried to blank her mind because he'd read it too well. "Nothing."

"You looked lost for a moment."

Not lost, she wanted to say. *Not when I'm with you.* But she couldn't. It was too soon. The feelings were taboo. He was her *boss.*

Still, any thoughts of boss and employee, of too soon or not soon enough, evaporated as he leaned still closer. "Emily, I don't know what it is about you."

His lips were just a breath from brushing hers. "I don't know what it is about *you,*" she whispered back.

His arm went around her, strong and protective. She nestled into it as if she belonged there…as if she belonged with him. When he tightened his embrace, his eyes were serious. But his mouth was curved in a small smile as if he were anticipating everything they were about to do.

She felt that same breath-hitching expectancy. The wait for his kiss was life-changing. In that moment, she put her divorce behind her. She took the present in her hands and hoped for a future that could include Jared. Her thoughts surprised her, almost as much as the touch of his lips on hers.

So many sensations bombarded her at once. The pressure of his lips was firm. The texture of his skin was taut and warm. The hunger behind his first touch was restrained, yet pulsing to be let loose. She readied herself for it. Then she realized, she couldn't be ready for it.

As his mouth opened over hers, as he demanded a response, as she got lost, she couldn't think about what she was doing. All she could do was give back whatever he asked. When his tongue stroked hers, she eagerly met each exploration. When he angled his head a little differently, her hands rose to his shoulders and then brushed into his hair. She held on to him so he could take her wherever he wanted to go.

He couldn't seem to get enough. She could feel her skin getting hotter, her cheeks flushing to match his level of arousal. They were both revved up and ready for more. But when his hands moved to her waist and inched her blouse out of her waistband, reality became a pressing concern. As soon as his hand touched the skin of her midriff, she wanted nothing more than to let him finish what they'd started. Yet she knew she couldn't. This was her boss. She needed her job, secret or no secret, and she'd just put it in jeopardy. How could she get out of this situation without looking like a foolish teenager who didn't know what she was doing?

But just as Jared had seemed to read her before, his hand slid away from her, his tongue ceased exploring and his mouth—although his lips clung a little—broke off their kiss. She heard his rough sigh.

Then she opened her eyes to gaze into his.

He turned from her slightly, rubbed his hand over his chin, shifted away, then focused on her. "I shouldn't have done that."

It seemed as if the words were hard for him to say, as if he didn't want to say them but knew he had to.

"I shouldn't have let you."

"It will *not* happen again," he said as if reassuring himself of that. "This isn't an excuse, but I've never met anyone who understood that moment of birth like you do." He rubbed his hands on his thighs. "This won't affect our working relationship. I mean, you don't have to worry about your job."

That was a relief but didn't address the attraction still simmering between them. "We can't pretend it didn't happen."

"No, we can't. I'll remember it every time I look at you. But I can control my actions." He glanced toward the kitchen and the message machine. "Did you get any phone calls tonight from Chloie Madison?"

"No, I didn't."

He looked troubled.

"That's your cousin?"

"Yes. I need her tomorrow."

Should she offer to help or not? Should she step in deeper or move away?

Yet, thinking about how she'd loved taking care of Amy and Courtney, she offered, "I can help." But perhaps her help wouldn't be wanted after what had just happened. "My day off is tomorrow," she reminded him. "I can look after the girls if you need me."

She saw in his eyes that he needed her in a much more basic and intimate way. But then the spark of desire diminished and control took its place.

She added, "I usually just run errands on my day off. But after what just happened, I'll understand if the situation is too awkward."

He seemed to think about the pros and cons. "The truth is—I'm surprised you're still here."

Emily certainly couldn't say she didn't run from problems. That's exactly what she'd done with the whole mess in Corpus Christi and her divorce. But she liked to think she was mature enough to face a problem without turning away from it. "What happened between you and me doesn't have to affect me watching your girls. You have surgeries in the morning and won't even be here."

"I'm interviewing a nanny in the afternoon, but that's at my office. Are you sure you'll feel comfortable with this?"

Jared Madison demanded honesty. She'd learned that over the months she'd worked with him. "I like Courtney and Amy. I'll be comfortable here."

He nodded and pushed himself up from the sofa away from her. "All right. I'll take you up on your offer. But I've got to tell you, I don't like being in debt to anyone. I'll pay you. Your time is valuable, too."

"No," came out of her mouth before she had time to think about it. "I don't want any payment. Let's just say we're doing this friend to friend."

After he studied her again, really studied her, he nodded. "All right. For now. But I *will* find a way to repay you."

She really didn't want him to repay her, and she suddenly realized why. The crush she'd had on him, if she could call it that, was turning into something else. Now that she was getting to know him, could she be falling in love with him?

That question scared her too much to even consider.

The following afternoon, Jared tapped his loafered foot under his desk, impatient though he shouldn't be. This woman sitting across from him could be Courtney and Amy's next nanny, although he couldn't quite imagine it.

"You've lived in Lubbock all your life?" he asked Mrs.

Brunswell, a sturdy woman in her early fifties with gray hair that stood out around her head like a fuzzy halo.

Very straight in her chair, she answered him, "Yes, all my life. I've no desire to go anywhere. Some people want to see the world. I make myself happy right here in Lubbock."

Would she curb the girls' curiosity about the world? Would she make them think Lubbock was all there was? On the other hand, it was good to be happy where you were. He was second-guessing himself, trying to find the perfect person to take care of his daughters. If he had to admit it, he'd already found her. *Emily* would be perfect. But she had a job that he knew was important to her, even though he wondered if she wouldn't be better suited working in the hospital, helping to deliver babies.

The older woman sat forward in her chair. "You said you have twins, Dr. Madison. The first thing to do with twins is to show them that they are individuals. It's much better not to dress them alike and not to let them spend all their time together. They also need to explore individual talents. If one takes piano lessons, the other should take clarinet. They deserve their own instrument. Do you know what I mean?"

Courtney and Amy liked to dress alike. They didn't have to. They had plenty of clothes in their closets, but they chose to wear the same outfits on the same days. They liked to be with each other. They played with other children and would be doing more of that when preschool started next week. But they preferred each other's company. Should he really interfere with that? What would Emily think?

He moved to the next point on his checklist. "In my occupation I have unusual hours. Would you be able to cook supper for them if need be?"

"I can cook, but I don't make chicken nuggets and

French fries. I cook good meals—pork and sauerkraut, spinach and zucchini casseroles, lots of vegetables, good protein, few potatoes. I have to cut out those carbohydrates, you know."

Jared thought about Emily serving the takeout food. He thought of Emily, helping cut Courtney's meat. He thought of Emily retying the bows in Amy's hair. What kind of meals would Emily cook if given the chance?

In spite of the restraint he'd been employing ever since last night and their earth-shaking kiss, he'd tried to keep his mind strictly on the practical aspects of his day. But he could not just drop that kiss from his memory. He couldn't just push it into a closet and lock the door. It kept peeking out. It kept unsettling him. It kept reminding him he was a man with needs. Just thinking about it aroused him and that had to stop.

Pork and sauerkraut. Spinach. Caring. Playing. Connecting.

"Do you know children's games?" he suddenly asked.

"I can play gin rummy and crazy eights," Mrs. Brunswell replied, as if those were the only games required.

"I'm thinking of outside games, too—hide-and-seek, scavenger hunts."

"Oh, I suppose we could do those."

Fair or unfair, he was getting the feeling that Mrs. Brunswell might keep an eye to the TV while she played crazy eights with her charges. She looked slow-footed to him as if running after a child would take a great deal of effort.

Jared's cell phone beeped and he was glad for the interruption. "Excuse me," he said to Mrs. Brunswell. Then swiveling away from her, he checked the number. It was Emily. "What's wrong?" he asked, worried.

"Nothing's wrong. The girls are fine. I'm fine. We're

having a great day. Two things," she said quickly. "First of all, your cousin Chloie called."

"Why didn't she call my cell?"

"She just got around to checking her messages and didn't have your number in her contact list. The good news is she can help you. She's on South Padre Island meeting with a client and will be back tonight. She can take care of the twins tomorrow. She said she's caught up on her Web design deadlines and can take a break."

"Thank goodness," he muttered, glad he didn't have to find a nanny right away. "And the second?" Hearing in Emily's voice the sweetness, caring and enthusiasm, he knew he could never hire Mrs. Brunswell.

"Second," Emily went on, "I'd like to take the girls to the park this afternoon. I'll be very careful with them, keep my eyes on them all the time. The fresh air would be good for them."

He suddenly realized he trusted Amy and Courtney with Emily because they couldn't stop talking about her, because of the expression on her face whenever she was with them. Whatever the reason, it was gut instinct. His gut instinct was telling him to dismiss Mrs. Brunswell. If Chloie could watch the girls until his mother was on her feet again, he wouldn't need to hire a nanny. "The park will be fine. I'm going to check in on my mother and then I'll be home."

After he closed his phone, he concentrated on Mrs. Brunswell again, searching for the words to tell her he wasn't hiring her.

Emily felt like a mom and loved the feeling! With the Texas-bright sun peeking around the clouds, she helped Amy from the swing, then took her hand and Courtney's.

They walked through the grass to the merry-go-round. Although she felt like a mom, she wasn't. Soon Jared's daughters would be under someone else's care. "You'll be playing with Chloie soon. That should be fun."

"Are you going away like our mommy did?" Amy asked.

This was dangerous territory. Emily didn't know enough about the situation to speak with the girls about it. At three and a half, how much could they remember about their mother?

"I'm not going to go away. I'm going to go back to working where your dad works."

"Mommy ran away and never came back," Courtney informed Emily seriously.

Was that how Jared had explained their mother's absence? Had they heard adults discussing it? She didn't believe Jared should just let them think their mother went away and never came back. Yet Emily knew she had no right to discuss this with them.

"Is Grandma coming back?" Amy wanted to know as they reached the merry-go-round.

"Your grandma hurt herself and has to have an operation. She might have to go to a special hospital for a little while before she can come home."

Courtney and Amy exchanged a glance as if this had been something they'd been worrying about. These two had a special bond and Emily hoped it would last throughout their lives. She'd often wished for a sister. She'd lost her dad to a construction-site accident when she was in high school. Her mom had died of an aneurysm a year before she and Richard had married. Looking back at her life, Emily wondered if she'd worn blinders and hadn't seen Richard's faults because she didn't want to be alone in the world, because she'd wanted to cling to that one person who was supposed to always stand beside her. But he hadn't. And by the time the lawsuit had been resolved, she'd realized how different their values were.

After Emily pushed the girls on the merry-go-round, they tried out the jungle gym while she sat on a concrete bench and watched. Suddenly a deep male voice behind her said, "They look as if they're having fun. Maybe I should get some equipment like that for the backyard."

Emily swiveled on the bench and looked up into Jared's penetrating green eyes. He was studying her loose-fitting red blouse and jeans, and she felt as if he were seeing more than her outside appearance. He'd apparently left his suit jacket in the car and rolled up his shirtsleeves. His tie was pulled down a little and the top button of his shirt open. Could he possibly know how sexy he looked, standing there with the sunshine gleaming on the russet strands in his dark-brown hair?

She returned her attention to the girls. "I think they'd enjoy a play set in the backyard."

Angling around the bench, he sat beside her.

They were silent for a few moments; then he commented, "It's been a long time since I've sat in the sun and watched them play. I think I've forgotten how to relax. I'm usually getting them dressed, feeding them, rushing off somewhere."

"You don't have to rush off somewhere now?" she asked.

"Not for a few hours. I have to return to the hospital later to check on patients. Can you stay through the evening?"

The more she was around Jared, the more she wanted to be around Jared. "I can stay."

"Good, then why don't I cook us an early dinner?"

"You cook?"

His eyebrows shot up. "You doubt me?"

"No, but are we talking about more than hot dogs or scrambled eggs?"

He laughed. "How about chicken Alfredo? We'll stop off at the market on the way home and get what we need."

"You shop, too?" she teased.

He shook his head. "I can see someone's been giving you a mistaken impression of grown men."

She went quiet.

"Your ex-husband didn't shop?"

"No, he relied on me for that."

After a few heartbeats, he asked, "How long were you married?"

"Six years. I met Richard when I was working toward my nurse practitioner certification."

Jared stared straight ahead, his gaze on his twins as he asked casually, "Have you dated since your divorce?"

Was he personally interested or just making conversation? "No, I haven't dated. I've been trying to get my life back on track." She waited a few moments, then took the opportunity to ask, "Have *you* dated?"

"No, I've been too busy to think about it."

Now he turned to study her, his gaze steady on hers. She read the flicker of desire in his eyes, a hunger that told her he was telling her the truth. It had been so long since a man touched her intimately, since a man had kissed her like Jared had kissed her last night. On second thought, she'd never been kissed like that before.

"There's chemistry between us," he said simply.

"I know."

"It's hard to ignore."

They both had agreed to do that. But with her just sitting here beside Jared, her attraction to him and his to her was palpable.

She saw a shadow pass over his face. "What?" she asked softly.

"I was thinking about how my marriage ended. Valerie couldn't accept the time I spent away from home. She hated the phone ringing in the middle of the night. Our plans were disrupted lots of times by my work, and I can understand how that disappointed her. My profession was the reason why we divorced. It's an obstacle to any relationship."

Emily absorbed that, then suggested, "Unless the woman you're dating understands."

There was a longing in Jared's eyes now. Maybe it was the longing to believe her. Maybe it was the longing to have a mother for his children. Maybe it was a longing he didn't believe he could ever satisfy.

Maybe, she guessed, he was sorry he'd brought up the subject because suddenly he stood and called, "Amy! Courtney! Let's go home. Too much sun and you'll look like red beets."

Emily smiled as the girls giggled. The tension between her and Jared eased. Yet she couldn't stop thinking about his kiss. Would a second kiss be even more potent than the first?

She might never know.

Chapter Three

Emily felt odd walking beside Jared down the grocery store aisles. He was acting as if this were an everyday occurrence! Her heart raced every time he glanced at her.

In the pasta aisle, he asked, "Angel-hair pasta or linguine?"

How could that question be so sexy on a man's lips? Their eyes locked for an interminable moment as the twins scampered around them.

Her mouth suddenly dry, she replied, "I like linguine."

"Do you have Italian in your soul?" he drawled, his Texas upbringing obvious.

Before she could answer, Emily's cell phone rang. She checked the caller's name. "It's Francesca," she murmured.

Leaning close to her, close enough that she could breathe in the scent of his musky cologne, Jared said, "If you need privacy, we'll keep shopping and meet you at checkout."

Emily was so tempted to touch the beard shadow on Jared's jaw…to straighten the collar of his shirt. But that freedom wasn't hers. Grateful that he understood her need for privacy, she stood still as he moved down the aisle and she answered her call.

"Francesca? Is something wrong?"

"No, nothing's wrong. Tessa and I wondered whether anything was wrong with you. I've hardly seen you for two days. We were beginning to worry."

"I left you a note on the refrigerator that I'd be taking care of Dr. Madison's twins," she protested, feeling defensive.

"I know. But it's not like you to be out of touch. Are you having fun?" her friend asked, less concern in her voice now.

"Actually, I am. They're two adorable little girls. He's done a good job raising them. He and his wife were divorced before she died, but he doesn't seem to want to talk about it."

"So what are you doing now?"

"We're shopping at the grocery store. He's going to cook for me and the girls tonight."

"Cook for you?" Francesca hesitated a few moments, then asked, "Is something happening between you and Jared?"

"I don't know," Emily responded honestly. "But for now, we're just being practical. He's going to cook and I'll probably end up with the cleanup."

"You're staying the evening?"

"Do you miss me so much?"

Francesca was quiet and Emily knew something was on her mind.

"What?" Emily asked.

"It's about Jared…."

Emily knew Francesca was hesitating because she didn't like gossip any more than Tessa or Emily.

Emily waited.

Finally Francesca said, "I've heard he has no time for anything serious…that his divorce really affected him and that the last thing he wants is to get involved with anyone long term."

"He has his daughters to think about," Emily replied quietly.

"Yes, he does," Francesca agreed. "I just don't want to see you get hurt."

"I haven't taken many risks in my life," Emily admitted.

"And you want to now?"

"It's too soon to tell."

"You know you can call on me or Tessa if you need us."

Emily did know that.

She checked on Jared's progress. He'd just reached the checkout line. "I'd better go."

"Have fun. But stay safe."

Emily's throat closed a little at her friend's concern. "I'll try."

A few seconds later, Emily hunkered down beside Amy, who was reaching for candy bars. "Do you really think your dad would want you to have *three?*"

Jared heard Emily's question and raised his brows at his daughter. He lifted his index finger. "One candy bar. You and Courtney can share it. Okay?"

Amy flashed him one of her best grins.

As he helped the clerk put the groceries into a bag, he asked Emily, "Did Francesca think you were abducted by aliens?"

"Not abducted. She was afraid I went willingly."

He laughed out loud. "Thank you, Emily. I don't know when the last time was I really laughed."

"You laugh with the girls."

"That's different." His shoulder bumped hers as they transferred bags to the cart. "I'm glad I'm getting to know you better."

"I'm glad I'm getting to know you…and Courtney and Amy," she added hastily.

But the intense look in his eyes and the tightening of his jaw told her there was something going on here between the two of them that had nothing to do with his daughters.

On the way out to the car, Jared carried the bags. Emily held Amy and Courtney's hands as they crossed the parking lot. She held on firmly.

Suddenly, right in front of them, a car's backup lights flashed, signaling the driver was backing up.

Emily swung the girls to the side out of danger.

Jared hurried to her. "I didn't see his backup lights at first. Sometimes I'm in too much of a hurry. Thanks."

The gratitude in Jared's eyes drew her closer to him, to the pull that was so strong between them.

Emily was struck by the stark difference between Jared Madison and her ex-husband, Richard. Jared thought about the people around him before he thought about himself. He didn't hesitate to say "thank you." She could probably count on one hand the times Richard had said "thank you" during their marriage, and she wasn't exaggerating. Richard had expected things of her. He'd expected her to act in a certain way, have sex when he wanted it and play the hostess when his work demanded it. Gratitude and appreciation never entered into it.

"What?" Jared asked in a low voice as if they were the only two people in the parking lot.

"Nothing," she murmured, knowing this wasn't the right time to reveal details of her marriage.

"I don't believe that was a nothing that crossed your mind, but I'll let it go for now." Moving toward his sedan, he pressed the remote to open the doors.

Why did Jared Madison move her so? How would he react if she revealed everything about her past?

After today, they'd probably both go their separate ways. His cousin would be taking care of the girls until he could find a nanny or until his mother was on her feet again. Emily would be put back into her colleague slot. She realized that definitely wasn't where she wanted to be.

An hour later, Jared asked, "What do you think?" as he offered her a taste of the sauce on a wooden spoon. He had changed into a Dallas Cowboys T-shirt and boot-cut jeans.

And she was having trouble keeping her mind on what he was cooking, rather than him.

He held the spoon while she took a taste, all the while her gaze on his. The heat she felt came from the two of them, not the electric burner.

"It's delicious," she managed to say, then added lightly, "You might have to give me cooking lessons."

He gave her a wry smile. "My repertoire is limited."

"Did your mom teach you?"

His shoulders stiffened. "No. When I was in med school, I either had to learn to cook or starve."

"Does your mom cook along with taking care of the girls?" Emily was trying to get a sense of his life.

"Most of the time. I give her a break on weekends if I can." He stirred the sauce thoughtfully, and after a glance at her, he went on. "I told you my marriage broke up because of the long hours and my profession. I was just wondering. What broke up yours?"

Terror struck Emily because the obvious reason her

marriage ended had been the lawsuit brought against her. Yet as she took a calming breath before replying, she realized the root of her problem with Richard had been something else.

Jared's voice turned gentle, his eyes serious. "You turned so pale. Was your husband abusive?"

She didn't want to give Jared the wrong impression. "No, he wasn't abusive. But he was…I think he felt entitled. When we got married, he felt entitled to certain privileges. He felt entitled to being superior over me. At first we both had our jobs and I played the trophy wife whenever it suited him. But then the—" She stopped abruptly. She'd been about to say that the lawsuit had changed everything.

"Go on," Jared prompted.

She shook her head. "I'm making it sound as if it were all his fault. It wasn't. I think the trouble we went through made us realize we wanted different things in life. My dad died when I was in high school and I missed him. I think I married Richard hoping to replace that hole in my life."

"Was your husband older?"

"Just five years. But enough that when I met him, I felt like the naive one, the one who could learn from him about a world I'd never seen, about a world I didn't know— corporate America and all that."

Jared stirred the sauce again, then gazed at her through the wisps of steam. "I can't imagine you as a trophy wife."

She laughed. "Now it's hard for me to imagine, too."

Still, Jared wouldn't let her escape from serious to light in the space of a moment. "This man you married must have been blind not to have seen the independent woman underneath."

"You're kind."

"I'm honest."

Yes, he was, and she felt as if she were keeping something important from him. Yet if she told him, wouldn't everything change? She'd had enough changes lately and wasn't going to run breakneck speed into this one. Francesca had warned her that she needed to be careful.

The dinner was delicious and the girls seemed to enjoy it, too, especially winding the pasta onto their forks. Emily showed them how to catch it with their spoons and they giggled throughout the whole process. After they finished eating, it was time for them to get ready for bed. Emily knew, as with most children, that could take a while.

She told Jared, "You cooked. I'll clean up. That's only fair."

Jared's smile showed his appreciation as he took the girls into their room.

Emily was drying the huge spaghetti pot when the twins came running out to the kitchen.

"Daddy said we could say good-night and we can give you a hug, too," Amy added.

Settling the pot on the counter, Emily hugged each of them, warmth filling her heart. Yet she felt an aching, too. She longed to have children of her own...to be a mom.

After she kissed them both good-night on top of their heads, they ran back to their dad.

When Jared returned to the kitchen, he asked, "How about a pot of coffee? I have about a half hour before I have to leave, unless you want me to get going so *you* can leave sooner."

She enjoyed his company so very much. "No. Coffee would be great."

"My mother's into specialty flavors. Not my thing, but it's all we have right now. Chocolate caramel or cinnamon mocha?"

"Chocolate caramel."

"That's her favorite."

"Are you worried about her?"

"Sure. But I'm optimistic, too. She's strong and healthy. She just landed badly."

"I'll bet she's scared."

"Of the surgery, you mean? Mom's not scared about much. She's a tough lady. How about yours? You said your dad died when you were in high school. What about your mom?"

"I lost her before I got married—an aneurysm."

"I'm sorry."

She still missed her mother a lot. The memories would come in waves, making her sad but giving her fond remembrances, too. "I truly felt like an orphan after she died. Sometimes I think we need our parents as much when we're adults as when we were kids."

An undecipherable look passed over Jared's face. She sensed a reserve in him about his mother, maybe even the possibility that they didn't get along. What could be the reason? She took care of his children, so he must trust her. Did he not want to depend on her?

Apparently the subject had become too personal, because he turned away from it and away from her, snagging two mugs from a mug tree. Soon they'd carried their mugs into the great room and settled on the sofa, a few inches apart.

"So, tell me about growing up in Lubbock," she said to make conversation.

His mouth tightened into a thin line. He set his mug on the table in front of them. "Growing up was growing up."

"If you don't want to talk about it, that's fine."

He ran his hand through his hair. "No. Sorry. I didn't

mean to snap. Probably growing up in Lubbock wasn't much different from growing up in Corpus Christi. Without the beach, of course."

"Brothers or sisters?"

Again he frowned, and she had the feeling she'd better stop asking questions or he'd clam up and not tell her anything.

But he answered her. "No brothers or sisters. But I always had good friends until I returned here to practice and got too busy to make them again." He laid his arm along the back of the sofa, and his fingers almost touched her hair. Not almost. He *was* touching her hair. "I like when you wear your hair loose rather than in a ponytail or a bun."

"Loose just doesn't seem professional for work."

His fingers were in the curls now, sliding through them, testing their texture. Then as if he realized what he was doing, he stopped. "I'd forgotten how nice an evening could be, doing something other than consulting on a case. You're easy to be with, Emily."

She didn't know quite what to say with him sitting there so close, the scent of male cologne tempting her closer. His muscled upper arms were evident under his T-shirt. His long legs were angled slightly toward her, his booted feet reminding her he *was* a Texan. Easy wasn't the word that came to her mind. They had to work together. If they took this any further—

A child's scream rent the air.

Jared was up and off the sofa so fast he disappeared into the twins' room before Emily was even in the hallway.

She hurried after him. Amy had awakened and was wide-eyed. Jared was at Courtney's bedside, not attempting to wake her.

Emily sank down beside Amy on her bed.

Courtney was sweating and Emily could tell she was breathing fast. Her eyes were wide open, but she appeared not to see her dad. Jared had sat down on the bed next to her, untangled the sheet from her arms and was stroking her hair. As Courtney cried, the sound broke Emily's heart.

Emily wasn't sure how long she sat there watching, wishing the episode to end for Courtney's sake, as well as Jared's. Amy had curled up beside Emily, and she found herself murmuring to her, "She'll be okay."

Amy nodded, maybe knowing that more surely than Emily.

Finally, after what seemed like hours, which might have only been fifteen minutes, Courtney turned into Jared's shoulder and her crying ceased. He kept stroking her hair comfortingly. While he still murmured consoling phrases, he tucked her in. When Courtney was sleeping peacefully once more, he kissed his daughter's forehead.

Emily stood, made sure Amy felt cared for and tucked in, too, and met him out in the hall. "That is so scary. Not just for her, but for Amy...and you."

"Usually Courtney doesn't remember anything about it. I consulted with a sleep psychologist. She said not to wake her, just comfort her and help her return to sleep when she seems ready. This happens more when she's overtired before she goes to bed."

"Was it my fault?" She'd played with the girls in many different activities.

"No, it just happens, usually in the first few hours after she goes to sleep."

"How long will this last?"

"I was told that most children outgrow them as they get older."

"Seeing one in progress is much different than reading about it on the Internet."

"I know, and I was worried about Amy seeing them. But when I tried to separate them, Amy would sneak back into the room and sleep on the floor next to Courtney's bed. She's protective of her sister."

They began walking toward the great room. There Jared studied Emily. "I'm surprised you didn't leave the room."

"How could I? Amy needed to feel she was safe, too, and to know Courtney would be all right."

"Sometimes I don't feel as if I'm giving either of them enough."

"You're wrong about that. From what I've seen, you're a great dad."

For a few moments, he seemed to search for the truth in her eyes. He must have seen what she was really feeling.

Lifting her chin, he kissed her.

At first it seemed like a light kiss, maybe a thank-you kiss, maybe a no-one-has-said-that-in-a-while kiss. But as soon as their lips met, the sensual pleasure of kissing him again kicked up Emily's pulse. The kiss must have done the same to him. He wrapped his arms around her and brought her tight against him. His T-shirt and her blouse were thin barriers to all the heat they were generating. So much heat, so much desire, so much pent-up longing.

When he broke the kiss, he shook his head. "I never intended for that to happen again, but the chemistry between us seems more powerful than good intentions. I'll understand if you want to work under another doctor in the practice rather than me."

"I don't want to work for anyone else, Jared."

He looked relieved for a moment. Then the creases along his eyes deepened. "You have to understand something, Emily. The last thing I want to do is get involved with anyone."

Had his marriage been so rocky that he didn't want to consider marrying again? Had his divorce been so painful? Had he still loved his wife but she hadn't wanted to be married to a doctor?

Emily had her own doubts about the way she was starting to feel about Jared. Was it too soon after her divorce? Was she seeing qualities in him that weren't really there? How could she trust her judgment after Richard?

"You have a lot on your plate," she responded. "Your daughters, your mom, your profession. I'm trying to get my life back in order. I've only begun to build it again here. So we'll deal with this—" she waved her hand "—chemistry. We're adults. We hardly see each other in the office, except to go over patient charts."

"So all I have to do is go back to looking at you as a colleague again." His mouth quirked up at the corners.

"Right, and I'll just see you as my boss."

After a long studying appraisal, he broke eye contact and checked his watch. "I'd better get going so you can go home at a decent time."

Crossing to the counter, he picked up his car keys. "My cell number's on the refrigerator. Don't hesitate to use it if something happens. Courtney doesn't usually wake up more than once in a night."

"I'll just handle her like you did if she does."

He nodded and went to the door. After a last, prolonged look at her, he left.

Emily knew they were both deluding themselves. Chemistry wasn't easily kept under wraps.

Unless Jared wasn't feeling the intensity she was. If that was the case, then there was nothing to worry about at all.

* * *

Midafternoon the next day, Emily was escorting a patient to the desk to make a follow-up appointment when the door to the reception area opened. Jared's daughters came running in, followed by a striking blond woman who looked to be in her forties.

"Emily!" they cried when the twins saw her.

She stooped down to greet them. "What are you doing here?"

"See Daddy," Amy said with certainty.

Chloie extended her hand. "You must be Emily Diaz. I'm Chloie Madison, Jared's cousin. He asked me to bring the girls in because he might not get home until after they're in bed tonight."

Jared came out of his office and saw them standing in the hall. "Way past their bedtime," he said, and crouched down to tickle them both and give them a hug.

After he straightened, he explained to Emily, "My mother's having surgery this afternoon and I'm going over to the hospital for the rest of the day." He took the girls' hands and led them to his office. "You can tell me all about what you did this morning with Chloie. About fifteen minutes," he mouthed to Chloie.

She nodded.

Then he disappeared to spend some time with his daughters.

Chloie and Emily moved to an alcove in the hall. "Am I keeping you?" Chloie asked.

"No, I had a cancellation."

"I hear you witnessed one of Courtney's night terrors. Scary, isn't it?"

"Yes, it was. But Jared handled it so calmly."

"I've watched him a couple of times myself, so I think

I'd know what to do if she has one when I'm there. It still spooks me a bit, though."

"I'm concerned about Amy as well as Courtney," Emily said.

Chloie nodded. "That makes sense. She's connected to her sister in ways we'll never imagine. That's the way twins are."

"Did you and Jared grow up together?"

"Yes, we did. I was two years younger but we were friends and watched out for each other."

"Are you friends now?" Emily knew she was prompting a bit, prying too much maybe, but she was curious about Jared's life and his relatives.

"After Valerie died, he became a totally different person."

"In what way?"

"He put walls up where there shouldn't have been walls. He didn't try to reach former friends who lived here. He said all he cared about was doing a good job and helping his girls grow up strong."

"It's not unusual to withdraw when you lose someone you love. Even though they were divorced, he must have still cared about his ex-wife."

"It was the way he lost her," Chloie said.

"The way?" Emily questioned.

"I shouldn't say any more. You'll have to ask Jared about it if you want to know. Secrets have hurt Jared more than once in his life. That's why he doesn't trust easily and why he rarely lets anyone get close."

Rarely lets anyone get close. Emily wondered about her own secret and what effect that would have on Jared. Should she tell him now about what had happened in Corpus Christi?

She remembered their second kiss and how it had made

her feel…how Jared made her feel. Yet he'd clearly told her he didn't want to get involved.

Did *she?* Hadn't Richard shown her men walked away when marriage got hard? Hadn't he abandoned her when she'd needed him most?

If she was smart, she'd forget about getting involved with Jared at all. Finding another job wouldn't be all that easy. She liked her life here.

Yet something about Jared tugged at her.

The question was—would she give in to the tugging?

Maybe. But she'd also keep her secret to herself.

For now.

Chapter Four

Emily entered the surgical waiting room at the hospital and spotted Jared immediately.

She watched him as he walked to the rack on the wall, took out a magazine, flipped through the pages and slid it back into its place without really looking at it. Then he crossed to the window, stared out into the dusky twilight and jammed his hands into his trouser pockets.

She went to him, watching her reflection take form next to his, not knowing how he'd feel about her being here. "Jared?"

When he turned, he looked surprised. Then he scolded her. "You should be at home having dinner."

Maybe she should be—for more than one reason. She didn't belong here with him. Her heart would be safer at home. She wouldn't feel as if she should reveal anything about her life to him.

But after her last patient of the day, she'd thought about Jared sitting by himself, waiting for his mother to come out of surgery. No one should have to go through that kind of crisis alone.

"I wanted to stop in and visit Leanne and her baby." Jared had delivered their patient's little girl last night. "How's your mother?"

"She's in Recovery. I won't be able to see her for about an hour."

"You don't like waiting, do you?"

His mouth curved up a bit. "I suppose that's obvious. No, I don't. I'm used to taking action, not sitting and waiting for another doctor to do his work."

She glanced at the cup of coffee sitting on the table. "How many cups have you had?"

"I lost count. Maybe four. I shouldn't have had *any*. I'm ready to pace the room until I wear out the soles of my shoes."

"Do you want to take a walk? The air might help the caffeine buzz."

Two nurses passed by the doorway as he thought about it. "Are you sure you have the time?"

"My time's my own. Francesca's tied up with the Neonatal Unit."

"And you don't like going home to an empty house."

Was she that easy to read? "No, I don't. The truth is— it seems empty since Tessa moved out. I mean, we all work erratic schedules, but with three of us, someone was always there. I miss her." Emily shrugged and smiled. "But she and Vince are happy and they're in the process of adopting two wonderful kids."

"Didn't you say they just married recently?"

So Jared was one of those rare men who listened. "Yes, they did. But the adoptions were sort of in the works before they married. Vince had unexpectedly become legal guardian of his best friend's little boy, and Tessa had been on an adoption list. She got the call right before they married."

"That's a lot to take on."

"Their story's a complicated one, but they're exactly where they want to be."

Jared seemed pensive for a few moments. After he glanced out the window again, he decided, "I think I would like to go for that walk."

A few minutes later, they passed through sliding glass doors outside into the August evening. A breeze tossed the edges of Emily's collar. She and Jared turned simultaneously toward the sidewalk that led past a row of live oaks. Lampposts illuminated their way.

Suddenly Jared stopped and took her arm. "Thank you for coming by. I was getting really wound up and this is helping."

His fingers were hot on her skin. His touch sent a deliciously warm thrill through her. She felt breathless, her pulse quickening as she looked up at him and their gazes held.

The green of his eyes darkened and he blew out a breath. "I keep telling myself we're going to have a professional relationship and then you look at me like that."

"Like what?"

"Like you're thinking about whatever happens whenever we get too close."

Jared meant physically, but she knew the chemistry happened when they got close emotionally, too. She and Richard hadn't really connected emotionally. But she and Jared...

A bond was growing between them that she couldn't deny.

He released her arm. Emily missed the physical contact but she could think more clearly. They started walking again.

"I had a talk with Chloie," she offered.

Jared sent her a sharp glance. "About?"

"Amy told her I was there when Courtney had her night terror. Chloie just said she knew how frightening they could be and that she learned from you how to handle them."

His tone was strained as he asked, "Was she questioning why you were there?"

"Oh, no. Why would you think that?"

He walked in silence for a few steps. "I got the impression when Valerie and I divorced that Chloie thought we hadn't tried hard enough."

"What did *you* think?"

He grew pensive. "I think we hit a stone wall. I couldn't change my practice or my dedication to my patients. Valerie was a new mom with twins and I couldn't be there as much as she wanted me to be there to help her. I wanted her to hire someone to help, but she didn't want to do that. She made up her mind about the divorce without much discussion. Once Valerie decided something, there was no convincing her to change her mind."

He sounded bitter about that. Just because of the divorce? She couldn't ask more questions without prying, and she didn't want to do that. "Richard asked for our divorce and he'd made up his mind, too. But by that time, I knew we didn't have much left."

"Marriage is an ideal most couples can't live up to."

Darkness was gathering around them, creating intimacy even though they walked on the public sidewalk. Emily found herself adding in a lower voice, "If two people have the same values and goals and outlook, I think it can work. My parents were happily married. I thought *I* would be. But I think I wanted somebody to love more than I wanted to look at who I was and who Richard was and how we could fit together."

"You've given this a lot of thought," he observed.

"I didn't like failing. I had to figure out what went wrong, why we couldn't stick it out through…" She stopped, then finished with "the hard times."

He looked as if he might want to question her about what those times were, but he didn't and she was glad. This wasn't the time or place to go into what she was hiding from him.

"Chloie told me you used to play together when you were kids, but then you were out of touch for a long time."

"Yes, we were. We reconnected at my stepfather's funeral. She was his brother's daughter. We aren't blood cousins."

As they walked farther away from the hospital, the quiet night surrounded them. The wind picked up, whipping by them. That morning Emily had fastened her recalcitrant curls into a bun. Now the longer they walked, the more strands the breeze pulled free. She stopped for a moment to refasten a few.

Jared stopped, too, watching her. "Don't. Just let it free." He turned toward her just as she looked up at him.

"Damn," he muttered but reached down anyway and fingered a loose tendril. "Your hair is so touchable."

The compliment reached down inside her and warmed all of the cold places where Richard's put-downs had hurt most. She hadn't been admired for being a woman for a long time. And Jared's words felt good, but they also warned her that chemistry between them couldn't be stifled easily, maybe couldn't be stifled at all.

He proved that when he slowly ran his thumb over her cheek. She could have stood there all night letting him touch her and he looked as if he wouldn't mind doing it.

"Maybe we'd better get back," she said softly, knowing that was the safer thing to do.

"Maybe we should," he agreed almost reluctantly.

"I want to stop in and see Leanne and her baby," she reminded him.

He nodded and they turned around to return the same way they'd come. This time they walked in silence, the current that Jared's touch had created zinging back and forth between them.

What was it about this man that made her feel wild and passionate and free? How long had it been since she really felt free? Yet it was more than the sexual current between them she was attracted to. There was a gentleness about him when he dealt with his daughters. That was as sexy as his tall Texan look, his broad shoulders and his hungry kisses. Yet she could tell by his restraint when he'd ended them that he didn't intend to get more involved with her.

Why was she so drawn toward him when her marriage had turned out badly? Didn't she remember Richard's concern for his own reputation rather than what she was going through? She'd felt so raw when he hadn't comforted her. She'd felt so separate when he'd gone to cocktail parties and left her with the stress of the lawsuit. She'd felt so alone during much of her marriage. When her divorce had been finalized, she knew she'd rather be alone than risk being abandoned again.

But then she'd met Jared. He'd awakened every sensation she'd thought she'd put to sleep.

As they rose in the elevator to the maternity and nursery floor, he admitted, "Courtney and Amy miss you."

"I miss them." Amy's smile, Courtney's hug had made her feel as if her heart was expanding. Before her interaction with them, she hadn't realized how much she wanted to be a mom.

"Any luck with the nanny search?"

"I don't want just anyone. I want someone who can take care of the twins as if they were her own."

Emily knew exactly what he meant. It was obvious when adults were pretending to like children and when they really liked them. She and Francesca and Tessa really liked kids. They could all spend an afternoon with Vince and Tessa's little boy, Sean, and their little girl, Natalie, and have a roaring good time. And Emily loved stopping by the toy store to buy them gifts.

Jared led her to the nursery, first checking in with the chief nurse at the desk. They used their security cards to access the nursery. After they donned sterile gowns, masks and caps, they walked past the little cribs, some fitted with blue bedding, some with pink. Emily wanted to pause at each one of them to just stare and appreciate each miracle of life. That's what these babies were—miracles—each and every one of them.

"Do you stop in here often?" Jared asked her as he waited for her in front of a baby girl's crib. Leanne and her husband, John, had named their little girl Olivia. He picked up the sleeping baby and cuddled her in his long arm.

"Every time one of our patients has a baby."

He glanced at her, held her gaze for a moment. "You want to see the pregnancy to its conclusion."

Yes, she so much wanted to. She so much wanted to be a midwife again. That was really seeing a pregnancy to its conclusion. It was almost doing what Jared did. There was nothing in the world like it. But now she had doubts about her judgment. She had doubts about why a baby had died under her care. The Wilsons' lawyer had looked back at previous pregnancies and pointed out another patient that Emily had, at the last minute, sent to the hospital for a cesarean. After hours of testimony, and the investigation by the licensing board, the attorney had her believing she'd missed something there. By the time Richard had doubted she was the same woman he married, she hadn't been sure of her judgment in making any decision and taking care of anyone, let alone being the professional she'd always wanted to be.

But now, consulting with Jared during a woman's pregnancy was almost as good. She didn't want anything to jeopardize the happiness she'd found again in her work.

"When I listen to the heartbeat of a baby in a mom's womb," she responded, her voice betraying her emotions, "I can't wait to see who that little being is going to be. Don't you feel that way?"

His gaze passed over her, assessing what she'd asked. "I've never looked at it like that, but I suppose I do. I can't wait to catch that infant in my hands, let the parents know what they've created together and see which parent's features that baby has. For most couples, one of the happiest moments in their marriage is when their baby is born. I like being part of that."

She knew exactly what he meant, but she couldn't tell him she knew. She couldn't tell him she had delivered babies, too. She'd come across some doctors, some obstetricians who had looked at midwives, who had looked at *her,* as if she belonged in a medieval time—especially the midwives who attended home births. Jared couldn't be one of those doctors, could he?

Even if he was accepting of midwives, even though she'd been judged not guilty of any malpractice, the lawsuit had left a shadow that hung over her professional reputation. Maybe it always would.

"Do you want to hold her?" he asked, his eyes twinkling at Emily over his mask.

"I'd love to hold her," she replied softly.

As he transferred the baby to Emily's arms, they almost embraced. Jared's large hand supported the baby's head and brushed against her almost intimately as he laid Olivia in her arms. Emily went still inside as she concentrated on the precious bundle. Jared's hand slipped away. Cuddling the newborn, Emily crooned to her, welcoming her into the world.

The infant yawned and her pink, little lips settled into a perfect bow.

"Do you want children of your own someday?" Jared asked.

"I do," she answered truthfully, but then realized she didn't have to bear an infant to be a mother. She'd be perfectly happy mothering Jared's daughters.

The thought stopped her cold. She hadn't realized she was falling for Jared so completely. She hadn't realized how his twins had captured her heart.

She'd better not weave fantasies and dreams. He didn't want an involvement. She *shouldn't* take the risk.

Just as Emily laid Olivia back in her crib, a knot forming in her throat, Jared's pager went off. He checked the number. "It's my mother's surgeon. I'm going to go outside to call."

She watched Jared as he hurried into the anteroom, as he stripped off the protective gown and mask and cap, as he pushed the button on the sliding glass door to step outside the nursery. With a sigh, Emily looked down at Olivia and brushed her finger over the baby's little hand.

Were dreams of wedding bells and lace with a partner who was tender and passionate and who loved with all his heart a fairy tale that could never come true for her?

At thirty-two, she was too old to believe in fairy tales.

* * *

The house that Tessa and Vince had bought to begin their married life was a fixer-upper. But along with the first coats of paint and Vince's newly mastered skill of hanging wallpaper, the newlyweds filled the house with love.

On Saturday afternoon, Emily carried a tray with dishes of chicken salad and fresh fruit onto the wraparound porch.

"Where did Vince take the kids?" Emily asked as Francesca brought a smaller tray with their drinks outside also.

Tessa had arranged napkins and silverware on three side tables beside each rocking chair.

"The new fast-food restaurant has a play gym," Tessa explained. "He insists the kids have to have fast food at least once a month because it's an inalienable right."

The women laughed.

"How's Sean's shoulder?" Francesca asked.

"It's coming along. We knew it would be slow. He could be three or four before he has full use of his arm again. But he's a trooper. We do exercises with him every day."

When Vince had lost his best friend in an automobile accident, Sean's shoulder had been injured. Vince had brought the baby home to Sagebrush because there was a physician in Lubbock who specialized in that particular type of shoulder injury. The little boy's surgery had been a success, but recovery would take a long time.

"When are you going back to your practice?" Emily asked her.

"Not until February, at least. And then, it will only be part-time. Actually, Rhonda can't wait because then she'll have care of the kids again."

Emily knew Vince's housekeeper, Rhonda Zappa, was a wonderful nanny. She'd taken care of Sean full-time until Vince and Tessa had married.

"What's she doing with herself? I know someone who could use her right now." Emily suspected Rhonda would be wonderful with Jared's daughters.

"She's visiting her son in Austin. She decided to stay for two months and be Grandma every day for a while, instead of just on holidays."

"Speaking of taking care of children, tell us about Jared Madison's daughters." Tessa's tone was bland, but an arched brow asked lots of questions.

"They're wonderful. Definitely into the princess craze. Jared's a terrific dad and—" She stopped.

Tessa eyed her shrewdly. "Is there something you're not telling us?"

"No, not really."

"Emily…" Tessa prompted.

Emily had confided her whole story to Tessa and Francesca earlier this summer, so there was no reason to hold anything back now.

"I like him," she said in a rush. "I know I shouldn't, but there's this connection between us or something. He doesn't want to get involved and I shouldn't even be thinking about it. But whenever we're alone together—"

"Fireworks?" Tessa suggested.

Emily nodded, and then realized how absolutely quiet Francesca had been. She hadn't eaten a bite of her chicken salad. She was sipping a glass of water and staring out across the lawn as if deep in thought.

Emily laid her hand on the arm of Francesca's chair. "Is something wrong? You're quiet today."

Francesca looked from Tessa to Emily and took a deep breath. "I'm pregnant."

Emily was too surprised to speak. Francesca had been

single for so long, except for one steamy June night with saddle maker Grady Fitzgerald.

"How can that be?" Tessa asked bluntly. "You said he used protection."

"I don't know how it happened. We *did* use protection. Maybe the condom broke. I missed my period. I let it pass, thinking it was just my busy life and work. I've never been regular. Last week, I felt a little dizzy...I haven't been hungry, my breasts felt tender and all the symptoms came together. I used a pregnancy test and...I'm over two months pregnant."

"Are you upset or happy?" Tessa asked.

"I think I'm still in shock. I'm a doctor, for goodness' sake! How could this happen to me?"

Emily studied her friend's face. "Shock or not, how do you feel about having a baby?"

Francesca's face broke into a lovely smile. "I'm beginning to like the idea a lot. A baby to love and hold—"

"And diaper," Tessa added with a grin.

"And diaper," Francesca repeated. "My problem is, I don't know what to do about Grady. We have very different lives.... We *want* very different lives. He's all about family. I wanted to run away from mine. He loves his work making saddles but he's a laid-back, no-pressure kind of guy. My career is everything to me...of course with a baby, that will have to change some. But my work with newborns will still be important. It will give me and my child a life."

"*Your* child?" Emily asked.

Francesca frowned. "You know I have trust issues. You know I chose badly with Darren. I chose the kind of man I ran away from. How do I know Grady is what he seems? We had one night together."

She studied the front yard, then added, "I have to tell

him, but I don't know how and I don't know when. And the truth is, I need time to figure out what's best for this baby."

"Do you think he's the kind of man who will want a say in that?" Tessa asked.

"I have no idea. Just because he comes from a large family doesn't mean he wants to be a dad. Maybe I don't want him to *be* a dad. Maybe I'm hoping he'd rather walk away."

Emily admired Francesca's honesty and the way she could analyze her life.

"I never thought I'd find happily ever after, but I have with Vince," Tessa reminded them.

"You and Vince are different," Emily proposed. "You fell in love in high school and, although you both denied it, that love never quit."

"We thought of our past as a burden, not something that connected us. So if Vince and I can be so happy, maybe the two of you need to take a few risks and find out if you can be happy, too."

Take a risk. Emily almost panicked at the thought. In the past, she'd definitely opted for safe rather than sorry. But what had that gotten her? Life with a man who'd spent their money on a huge house and expensive toys that were supposed to promote his career? She'd supported his dreams and tried to make them hers. But that hadn't worked.

Could she trust a man to stand by her no matter what? To actually believe in marriage vows? To promise a lifelong commitment?

She knew Prince Charmings were in short supply. And she was no Cinderella! Tessa and Vince might be the exception rather than the rule.

When Emily exchanged a look with Francesca, she knew Francesca believed that, too.

Chapter Five

Emily hadn't seen Jared all day on Monday. That was a good thing, she told herself. If she didn't see him, she couldn't want to see him more.

Her luck ran out when she headed into the hall. There he was, coming out of his office, his cell phone at his ear. When he saw her, he ended the call and frowned.

"Is something wrong?" Maybe one of his patients went into unexpected labor. Maybe his mother had spiked an infection. Maybe his life was none of her business.

As he hesitated, she felt the urge to step closer to him. But she didn't have to. He took a step closer to her. "That was Chloie."

Although she felt current between them, although deep in his eyes she saw he felt it, too, she changed her focus to his twins. "Are Amy and Courtney all right?"

"Oh, they're fine. Except…they insist they want to see their grandmother."

"Does that surprise you?"

He slipped his phone into the holster on his belt. "No. I was just hoping I could sidetrack them, at least until she got to the rehab facility. But they know she's in the hospital and they want to see her. I don't think it's a good idea."

Emily thought about it. "You said they saw her fall."

"That's right. And they saw the ambulance come and take her away."

She tried to put herself in the twins' place. "They want to be reassured she's coming home again."

"I have been reassuring them of that, but I don't think they believe me."

Emily studied Jared. Already she suspected he was the type of man who liked to control his world. Once in a while, however, he had to settle for plan B. "What would be so terrible about taking them to the hospital for a short visit? They're well-behaved."

The lines around his eyes cut deeper with concern as he shook his head. "I don't want them to see anything that will scare them. Hospitals aren't always the kindest places. There are unusual machines, IVs…"

"I think you have to decide whether the benefits would outweigh everything else. What they conjure up in their thoughts could be worse than what they might actually see."

Now his green eyes assessed her, considering her suggestion. "You mean if they're excited about seeing their grandmother, they won't notice anything else?"

She smiled. "I'm not that naive. Did you ever think about buying them one of those hospital play sets and explaining equipment they might see before they go?"

"I knew there was a reason I hired you," he said with a teasing smile that sent her heart into an upbeat rhythm.

"The reason you hired me was to shift some of your patient load," she teased back, feigning offense.

"And that's worked very well," he said seriously. "Our mothers-to-be trust you. You've really added a lot to this practice."

The way he was looking at her with respect for her professional talent meant so much. "Thank you," she murmured, wanting him to know her whole story, yet still afraid to confide in him.

After they stood there gazing at each other for a few heartbeats, Emily felt that tempting tension rise between them again.

"Why don't you come with me to the toy store?" he suggested. "You can help me pick out the most appropriate play set."

She shouldn't. She absolutely knew she shouldn't. What about taking a few risks? her inner voice asked while Francesca's admonition to be careful played, too.

Jared took her silence as reluctance. His expression became serious. "You probably have other plans. The girls and I have taken up more than enough of your time."

"No, that's not true! I don't have any other plans. In fact, I had a message from Francesca that she'd be tied up at the hospital again tonight. So I'd like to help you pick out a play set." Maybe her concept of her world had to change. Maybe she had to take a step forward to *move* forward!

"Don't feel you have to come, Emily. I don't want you to feel any pressure."

"I don't feel pressured, Jared. I'd tell you if I did. The problem is, I like being with you."

"You like being with me?" His voice held surprise.

"Yes. You're a good listener. You're easy to talk to. And we seem to understand each other. All qualities I like in a friend." If she kept this light, maybe being with Jared wouldn't be a mistake. She knew she was falling for him, but if they could be friends, maybe the fall wouldn't hurt her.

"Friends, huh?"

She nodded as if that's all she expected or wanted. Being honest with herself, she knew she wanted a lot more.

They'd been standing about a foot apart and now he moved closer. "I don't think we're going to be friends like Chloie and I are friends."

"Probably not," she admitted. "Every friendship is different."

"What do you expect from your friends?" he asked, his voice husky.

What she wanted was to step into his arms. What she wanted was to feel his lips on hers again. And ultimately what she wanted was way more than he'd said he was willing to give.

What did she expect from friendship? "That depends on the level of friendship. It's come to mean something different since I moved here and met Tessa and Francesca. I guess loyalty is the main quality I expect."

The silence in the offices wrapped around them. The other doctors as well as the office staff had gone. No one was around but the two of them. If he reached for her, she wouldn't pull away. He looked as if he wanted to. He looked as if he liked what she expected of friendship.

But Jared was the type of man who thought about professional reputation and ethics and time and place.

Breaking eye contact and the sensual haze that always seemed to surround them when they were together, he reached into his pocket for his keys. "Would you like to ride with me to the toy store?"

Emily considered sitting next to him in his sedan, aware of him in the confined space. "I'll follow you."

Fifteen minutes later, Emily walked beside Jared through the rows of the toy store. She felt as if she were on a date, though she knew she wasn't. He'd tugged off his tie and opened the top button of his shirt. She could see a hint of his dark-brown chest hair. He was at least six feet tall and she felt almost fragile beside him. Every now and then, she caught the trace of a male fragrance that lingered at the end of the day. His thick hair curled slightly over his collar in the back and her fingers tingled to touch it. He glanced at her now and then. When their eyes met—

What was brewing between them was powerful chemistry neither of them could deny. Yet they were both trying to.

As they traversed the sports section, he stopped in front of the soccer balls. "I'm thinking about getting them one of these for Christmas."

"You're going to be a soccer dad?"

He shrugged. "I could take them to their games on Saturdays when I'm not on call."

He appeared nonchalant but she could hear his voice strain when he realized that he couldn't be with his daughters whenever they needed him.

After the sports aisle, they turned the corner into little-girl land. Emily pointed to a princess Barbie. "Now, *that's* a Christmas present."

Jared laughed. "I can see how being a dad colors what I buy for them. I might have to consult you as a personal shopper for Christmas."

She stopped at a miniature tea set with pictures of Cinderella on the pot and dishes and lifted it from the shelf. "Do you mind if I buy this for them?"

"You don't have to do that."

"I want to. I think they'd have fun with it. Tea parties are great for the imagination."

"I'm sure they'd like to have tea with *you.*"

From his smile and the sincerity in his voice, she could see he meant that. From the glimmers of desire in his eyes, she could also see that he found her attractive, and that was such a balm to her ego. "I was thinking of them having tea with *you,* along with their teddy bears and Barbie dolls."

"Now, *that's* a picture," he admitted with a chuckle.

They found the hospital play set easily in the dollhouse section. Jared examined it, nodding as he did. "This is a good idea, Emily. I'm glad you suggested it."

Emily's cell phone began playing a lilting tune. She retrieved it from the outside pocket of her purse.

Jared took the tea set from her so she wouldn't have to juggle it. When she checked the caller ID, she froze.

He studied the expression on her face and asked, "Emily?"

"It's my ex-husband. I'd better take this." Richard never called her. Since the divorce, they hadn't had much communication, although there were still a few loose ends to tie up. She sent him a check every month. If he was calling, there would be a reason. And he wouldn't stop calling until he got her. She knew her ex that well.

"Excuse me," she said to Jared as she walked to the end of the aisle where she had better reception and some privacy.

After she answered, her ex-husband asked, "How are you doing, Em?"

She didn't like the nickname, never had really. He hadn't taken her seriously when she'd told him that. "I'm okay, but this isn't a good time. Can I give you a call back later tonight?"

"You're still at work?"

"No, I'm not."

"On a date?"

Ever since their divorce, he hadn't cared. Why would he now? "No, Richard. I'm shopping."

"Well, it's good to know you have enough money to do that. Low expenses in Sagebrush."

"I'm getting by. I'm sharing a house and that helps." She didn't even know why she told him that except she wanted him to realize she didn't have a lot left over at the end of the month. "So, why are you calling?"

"I need your signature on something."

"What?" All of their belongings except two had been divided up.

"I want to sell the painting that's hanging over the sofa, but your name's on the provenance, too."

The only property that hadn't been completely settled was the painting and the boat, a thirty-six-foot sailing vessel that Richard used to impress clients. She wondered why he needed money, though. His salary had always covered their bills comfortably. They'd used her salary for her personal expenses and extras—parties, dinners out, half of the down payment on the boat.

"How do you want to handle selling the painting?" she asked, still mourning the loss of the relationship she'd begun with stars in her eyes, intending it to last forever.

"Do you have a fax?"

She didn't, but Francesca did. "I can give you my room-mate's fax number." She rattled it off.

"That's great. I'll fax the form over right away. Sign it and send it back to me by registered mail, okay?"

"Okay."

"Thanks, Em."

"No problem."

The awkward silence vibrating on the line came from two people who didn't know each other anymore, who maybe had never really known each other. "Take care," he said as if he wanted to say more but didn't know how.

"You, too."

After she closed her phone, Jared approached her. "Is everything okay?"

"Fine. My ex needs my signature. We bought this painting together for the living room…" She stopped, a lump forming in her throat.

"Everything has a memory attached, doesn't it?" Jared asked as if he knew.

She nodded, tucking her phone into its purse pocket, not meeting his gaze.

He set down everything he was holding onto the floor, then straightened, came very close and lifted her chin. "I was divorced, too, so I understand that even though a marriage is over, there are still remnants left of what it once meant."

She wanted to tell him everything—about how Richard had turned away from her during the court proceedings, about how his lack of support had left her feeling so alone. But there would be so much to explain…so much Jared might not understand.

"Do you still love him?"

The answer seemed to be important to Jared. Why was he asking? Because he wanted her to be free of entanglements? To be free of her past? She didn't know if she'd ever be free of that.

"The part of me that once loved him remembers what that was like. I wish him well. But no, I'm not still in love with him."

Jared searched her face, perhaps not knowing if he could believe her words. Why would he doubt what she said? Unless someone had lied to him before?

The intensity of the moment passed as his hand slid from her chin. He picked up the play set and the tea set he'd set on the floor. "I think you should come over and show the girls all the aspects of the hospital that they might see. Explanations wouldn't be too scary coming from you. I might be too clinical. What do you think?"

Her voice was soft with gratitude when she answered, "I think you're trying to distract me from the call. Thank you. I'd love seeing your daughters again."

"All right. Then maybe after you show them around the toy hospital, you can teach me the finer points of having a tea party."

His dry voice made her smile. He would do anything for his daughters. With sudden realization, she knew *she'd* do anything for him.

Yet once before she'd placed a man's concerns before hers. Once before she'd let Richard's ambition and desires supersede hers. And when she'd needed him—

When she was with Jared, she had to remember her failed marriage. Otherwise he could break her heart and she wouldn't be able to patch it up again.

Jared could have kicked himself for inviting Emily along home with him. Yet she had been good for his girls. And she'd looked so sad after her phone call.

Still, what about what was good for *him?*

For the past two years, he really hadn't thought about

himself. Amy and Courtney had needed him day and night. His career demanded his time day and night.

He'd been lonely after his divorce. And after Valerie died...

He'd been confused and in turmoil because she hadn't confided in him. What kind of man was he that she couldn't tell him the truth about her illness?

Since then he'd denied physical needs and fallen into bed exhausted every night. Work and spending time with the twins was like a numbing drug. He worked more and tried to meet their every need so he didn't have to think about a life he didn't have.

Yet why would he want a woman in his life again? Why would he want to complicate it? Why take the chance on a relationship that might not work out? He'd be putting Amy and Courtney at risk, too.

Still, as he stood in the kitchen supposedly pouring milk for Courtney and Amy while surreptitiously watching them with Emily, he knew life demanded more of him than work and child care.

Would sex be a start? Would an affair lead him to a life again?

The wind whistled against the house as he listened in on Emily's conversation. She was on the floor with the twins in the great room.

Courtney asked her, "Are there people in every room?"

"Yes, there are."

Jared watched Emily settle one of the dolls into the tiny bed.

She asked Amy, "Would you like to turn on the TV for this patient?"

Amy solemnly nodded.

Courtney pushed the miniature wheelchair into the patient's room. "The lady in the other bed needs this."

"Would you like to give her a name?"

Courtney thought about that. "Mrs.…." She looked around the room and her eyes fell on a vase with silk flowers. "Mrs. Flower."

"I like that name," Emily encouraged her. Then she picked up another doll dressed in a white uniform. "The nurse is coming in to give her medicine."

"Here's the doctor," Amy said proudly, picking up the next play figure. "Just like Daddy."

Jared had to smile. Hopefully Amy and Courtney could visit his mom without too many fears, without being scared by what they saw. Emily was so good with his daughters. And when he kissed her, he felt arousal that he hadn't experienced since his days at Texas Tech.

He took the glasses to the table along with cups of pudding, but he didn't call them yet. Rather he went over to the sofa where they were playing by the coffee table with Emily.

"What do you think of the hospital?" he asked them.

He could feel Emily's gaze on him and to his surprise, he liked the idea of her looking at him. There was respect in her eyes, maybe even admiration. Something else, too. That something else that made him want to kiss her whenever their eyes met.

"The hospital is big," Courtney decided.

In reality, it wasn't that big, only four floors, but to his daughters, the building would seem immense.

"You don't have to worry about getting lost or anything like that. When we go see Grandma, you can hold on to me," he assured her.

"And Emily."

He hadn't thought about Emily visiting his mother.

"Oh, I don't think I'll be going," Emily said, glancing at him, making sure she didn't overstep their working relationship or their friendship.

Friendship. Had he ever been friends with a woman?

Courtney ran to him, wrapped her little arms around him and looked up at him with big green eyes. "Daddy? Can Emily come, too?"

How could anyone say no to this beautiful child who had formed a bond with this woman who was caring enough to be a mother? Courtney liked Chloie, but she never responded to his cousin the way she responded to Emily. Neither did Amy.

Emily's cheeks were flushed as if she were embarrassed and didn't know what to say or do.

Stooping down, he lifted Courtney into his arms. "Can you tell me why you want Emily to come along? I'm sure she has a very busy schedule, so it has to be an important reason."

Courtney bit her lower lip as she thought about what he'd asked. "I won't be scared."

Jared had the feeling that sometimes when his daughters were with him, they thought he'd be called away and they'd be left alone. He didn't know how to counteract that. Apparently they felt more solid with Emily. That was a shocker.

"Why don't you two have your milk and play and I'll talk to Emily about it? Okay?"

Courtney nodded again, leaned toward him to give him a kiss on his cheek. Every one of those kisses was precious.

He carried her over to the table and settled her in one of the chairs, lifting the lid from her pudding. Amy ran over and he did the same for her. He left them jabbering about the hospital and patients.

Emily had risen from the floor. Tendrils of curls had

come loose from her ponytail and wisped around her face. Her color was still a little high. He couldn't seem to get enough of looking at her face, her sweetly curved lips, her long eyelashes that fringed her dark brown eyes and emphasized them.

"I don't have to go along. I certainly don't want to intrude on your time with your mother."

His time with his mother was always strained. With the girls around, less so. Truth be told, he wondered what his mother would think of Emily, and vice versa.

"The girls seem to find a certain level of comfort and safety when you're with them. I wouldn't want to take that away from them in a strange setting. Are you busy tomorrow evening?"

"No, I'm not busy," she admitted, realizing she didn't have a social life outside of her friendships with Francesca and Tessa. "But are you sure you want me involved? Would your mom want a stranger around?"

"I don't know what my mother will or won't want. I do know I'll keep the visit short. I don't want to overtire her, and the girls can be a handful when they get excited and start asking questions. That's where I think you'd be a big help. You have a calming effect on them."

"If I can help, I'd be glad to come along. But if for some reason your mother doesn't want any other visitors, I can wait out in the hall, or visit the nursery again."

He remembered too well the day he'd transferred Leanne Martin's baby to Emily's arms. She would make a wonderful mother. He could imagine her pregnant, getting larger with child each month.

Oh, no, he wasn't going there. He might be considering a night of hot sex, but a minister and wedding bells weren't on his agenda. He'd done that once. He'd been a lousy husband and back then, not a very good father. He'd been building his practice, and he'd left the needs of his infants to Valerie.

If he had it all to do over again, what would he change?

He didn't know. Valerie's distaste of his being called away had always caused problems between them. But those problems had turned into resentment on both their sides, and that colored everything they had done and said.

He could have done it differently. He should have been more understanding.

Valerie had received her diagnosis and decided she knew best—that he and the twins shouldn't be with her in her last days. If he'd been a better husband...if he'd been more understanding...then maybe she would have trusted him to be with her through it all. Even at the end.

"Jared." Emily looked concerned as if she'd asked him a question and he hadn't heard her.

"Do you want to go to the hospital as soon as we're finished for the day?"

"That would probably be best."

She studied him more closely. "Are you okay?"

"I'm fine. I was just considering what type of father I would be if I were in a different profession."

"Do you really think changing your career would make you a different kind of dad?"

She had a point there. "I'd have more time to give them."

She looked as if she wanted to say something, but was hesitating to say it.

"Tell me what you're thinking." The one truth he'd learned in his life was that honesty avoided much heartbreak.

"I'm thinking that even if we had all the time in the

world, we wouldn't have enough time. It's more important that you don't waste a minute of the time you have with them. If you're really present to them, if you care about what they're doing, that's what matters."

Jared suddenly realized that that was the reason his daughters liked being with Emily. When she was with them, she was with them. Nothing interfered with her concentration on them, and they felt special because of it.

He moved closer to her, thinking about the call she'd received from her ex-husband. The few things she'd told him had led him to believe her ex hadn't appreciated her at all. He glanced over at his twins and saw they were still occupied with the pudding and each other.

Letting his hand rest lightly on Emily's shoulder, he asked her, "Why didn't you have babies when you were married?"

She looked away and then back at him. "I wanted them. Richard wanted to wait until we were financially secure."

"And that day never came," he guessed.

"No, it didn't." She didn't elaborate, though he wished she would. Maybe in time.

Had he decided to spend more time with her for reasons other than his daughters?

Since Emily didn't elaborate about her marriage, he asked anyway, "What finally broke the two of you up? Usually there's that straw that breaks the camel's back."

For a moment, Emily looked absolutely trapped. Her face drained of some of its color. What could have been so horrible that she'd have this reaction?

"Emily?" He slid his hand under her hair and stroked her neck.

"There wasn't just one thing," she finally said. "He asked for a divorce and I knew…I knew we didn't have anything left."

What she was telling him could be true. But he suspected there was more. He could see it in the turmoil in her big brown eyes. Was Emily keeping secrets from him, too? And if she was, what was he going to do about it?

He heard the scrape of a chair on the wooden floor and the pitter-patter of Amy's sneakers as she ran over to him. She never seemed to walk anywhere.

"Can Emily read us a story before we go to bed?"

He stepped away from Emily, closer to his daughter. What did he really know about Emily Diaz? He knew what she'd given him in her résumé. He knew what her references had told him. Yes, she was a kind, compassionate woman who could relate to kids. And from his reaction to her, she turned him on in a way a woman hadn't in a very long time.

But did he know the essence of her? Did he know what made her tick? He suddenly wondered why she'd had to travel across the state to start a new life here…so far away from her husband.

The prize-winning question was—did he want the answers to all of his questions, or did he want to just concentrate on his daughters and his profession without muddying up his life with an affair?

"I think we've taken up enough of Emily's time. She has a roommate who hasn't seen much of her lately, and I'm sure she has things to do at home, too. Did you finish your milk?"

Amy nodded.

"Great. As soon as Courtney's finished, you can try to put your pajamas on all by yourselves."

Then he turned back to Emily and gestured to the play set on the floor. "Thank you for taking the time to find that with me and to play with them." His voice was more formal than he wanted it, but he had to draw a line in the sand.

He saw a flicker of hurt in Emily's eyes. He hated that. But he had to consider what he was doing very carefully. He had to make sure he made the right decisions this time for both his daughters…and himself.

Emily's shoulders squared a little as she told Amy, "Your dad's right. I have to be going. But I'll see you tomorrow evening."

Her purse was lying on the end table beside the sofa. She picked it up quickly and threw the strap over her shoulder. Then she stepped around the play set, crouched down before Amy and gave her a hug. Afterward, she headed for Courtney and did the same.

Jared walked Emily to the door. But he didn't touch her, and he definitely didn't kiss her good-night.

Emily had questions in her eyes as she said good-night and left.

But he didn't have any answers.

Chapter Six

Emily felt like an outsider the following evening as she walked beside Jared to his mother's hospital room. Courtney clutched Stardust under one arm as she held her father's hand. Amy had a grip on Emily's. She was sure his daughters wanted her here, but she wasn't sure at all that *he* did. She took a firmer grasp on the two bouquets of flowers she carried for the twins.

Outside the door, Jared leaned close, his breath warm on her ear as he assured her, "We don't have to stay long. In fact it would probably be better for my mother if we don't. I don't want the girls to tire her out."

The solemn expression on Jared's face, as well as his rigid bearing, told Emily the girls might not be the only reason he didn't want to stay long.

Emily handed a bouquet to Courtney and one to Amy.

Courtney held Emily's hand a little tighter as they neared the bed.

Gloria Madison pressed the control that raised her head so she was in a sitting position. She was a beautiful older woman with thick steel-gray hair that lay in soft curls around her face. Her eyes were green like Jared's and she was smiling at her granddaughters. "Come here, darlings. I've missed you."

"We brought these for you," Courtney said, giving her grandmother the flowers in her hand. Amy did the same.

Gloria bent and smelled them—carnations, daisies and roses. "How pretty! Thank you so much for bringing them. They'll brighten up my room." Her gaze went to her son. "I see you brought a reinforcement. Are you going to introduce us?"

"This is Emily Diaz. She works at the practice with me and has been helping with the twins. They wanted her to come along. Emily, my mother, Gloria Madison."

Emily went over to the bed and extended her hand. "It's so nice to meet you. The twins have been worried about you. They needed to see you were recovering."

"Did you convince my son to let them come?"

"It was his decision." Emily spotted an empty vase sitting on the windowsill. "Why don't I put some water in this and arrange the flowers for you?"

Jared removed folded pieces of paper from his shirt pocket. He gave them to Courtney and Amy. "They drew pictures for you, too."

Both Amy and Courtney opened up the folded pieces of paper, explaining to their grandmother what they had drawn. Their childish chatter filling the room brought a huge smile to Gloria's face.

While she chatted with her granddaughters, Emily

slipped into the bathroom and filled the vase with water. She was arranging the flowers when Jared stepped inside.

Instead of turning around, she sought his gaze in the mirror. He was standing behind her, tall and broad-shouldered, in a striped oxford shirt and casual slacks. She remembered his last kiss and being held in his arms. She wanted him to touch her and he looked as if he'd like to. But he kept a foot between them.

When she turned around to face him, that foot of separation disappeared. She just waited, their attraction for each other thrumming between them.

"Will you be all right here for a few minutes?" he asked. "I'd like to check on a patient."

"Sure. I'll be fine."

Cocking his head, he asked, "Are you always fine?"

"I try to be. I believe if I act as if I've got a handle on everything, then maybe I will."

"You're an optimist."

"You're just learning that?" she joked.

"Yes, I am." His silence said he was learning other things, too.

There was a glint in his eye, a spark of desire, the recognition that their attraction wasn't going to go away because they wanted it to. She found herself responding to it. Her heart was pounding and a butterfly did a flip in her stomach.

Finally Jared said huskily, "I won't be long." Then he left the bathroom, explained to his mother where he was going and strode down the hall.

Although she didn't know why, Emily felt shaken by their exchange. They were coming closer and closer to something inevitable. What? Confronting their attraction? Doing more with it? Yet Jared didn't want involvement.

She shouldn't get involved with a man who had walls around his heart. She was asking for heartache if she did.

Running the cold water, she took a paper towel and held it to her cheeks. Then she picked up the vase with the flowers and returned to Gloria. The older woman eyed her thoughtfully as Emily set the flowers on the windowsill.

Amy and Courtney had settled into a chair together with a magazine on their laps. It was one of those country magazines with pictures of farms and children and animals. They chatted to each other about them and then showed them to their grandmother. Once they were intrigued again by a picture of a huge dog in the magazine, Gloria laid her head against the pillow. "Jared doesn't trust many people with his daughters. He must think highly of you."

"I work with Jared as an obstetrical nurse practitioner. I hope he respects the work I do and knows what kind of person I am."

"Oh, I think he knows."

Emily's attention went from the girls, who were studying a wagon filled with pumpkins, to Jared's mother.

Emily didn't say anything, though. If Jared's mom had something she wanted to tell her, Emily would give her the opportunity.

"I think he's interested in you, and you like him," Gloria suggested.

What should she say? What *could* she say? After all, Jared's daughters were right there. Children had great hearing and long memories.

Something about his mother's intent green gaze made honesty essential between them. "We don't really know each other very well. In fact—" She stopped, realizing she was about to say too much.

"In fact?" Gloria urged her on.

"There's a lot about me that Jared doesn't know, just as I'm sure there's a lot I don't know about him."

"Time could take care of that," his mother assured her.

"Possibly."

Gloria appraised her for a few more moments. "My son has walled himself off to everyone but his daughters until now. When he looks at you, I see a change in him that wasn't there before."

Emily couldn't help but ask, "What kind of change?"

"Curiosity, appreciation, possibility. A small crack where a little bit of light is glimmering through. He needs a personal life. He hasn't had one since his marriage."

"I don't think he wants one," Emily admitted.

"You could be right. On the other hand, the crackle I see between the two of you might be bigger than both of you."

Crackle. Sizzle. Sexual chemistry. Even if they had that, did Emily want an affair? She'd never had affairs. She'd had one serious relationship—with Richard.

She had so much baggage. Sending a check to Richard every month was a responsibility she took seriously. It would take her years to cover the money he'd siphoned from his pension. What man would want to take that on? Not to mention the way Jared might feel when he knew the circumstances behind her legal bills.

"How old are you?" Gloria asked.

"I'm thirty-two."

"Have you ever been married?"

"Yes, I'm divorced." She expected to see judgment in Gloria's eyes, maybe disapproval. To her surprise, she didn't see either.

"And Jared is forty-three, also divorced. I imagine you both have history that needs to be put to rest."

"Sometimes history can't be put to rest." Not when it was ongoing, Emily thought…not when she felt as if she had to hide it.

"Would you do something for me, Emily?"

"What?"

"If you have feelings for Jared, don't give up on him if he seems to push you away."

Courtney suddenly scrambled off the chair and placed the magazine into her grandmother's lap. "See the horse? I want to ride a horse."

"Me, too," chimed in Amy.

Emily was glad for the interruption.

While the girls chatted with their grandmother again, she had time to think about their conversation. The last thing she'd expected to find in west Texas was romance. Yet Jared was the type of man she'd always dreamed of meeting someday. He was sexy and caring and a wonderful dad.

There were so many things he didn't know about her.

When Jared returned to the room a short time later, Emily was sitting in the chair with Courtney on her lap. Amy was standing at her grandmother's bed, singing a song she'd learned in preschool.

Emily noticed Jared stop in the doorway, taking in the scene. His gaze was gentle as it rested on his daughters. But when it settled on his mother, he frowned and a distant look came into his eyes. Emily had noticed that same distance in his tone when he mentioned his mom, and couldn't help but wonder what had caused it. Gloria Madison seemed to be a kindly, friendly woman. What had transpired between mother and son to cause resentment? Was that what Jared felt toward his mother?

Crossing to Gloria's bed, he said, "I think two little girls are more than ready for bed."

"We're not sleepy, Daddy," Courtney told him, and then yawned.

He laughed. "Even if you're not sleepy, Grandma needs her rest, too."

"It was so good to see you." Gloria gave both Amy and Courtney hugs. To Emily she said, "I'll be going to a rehab facility tomorrow, but I'd love to see you again."

"I enjoyed talking to you. I'll visit you if I can." The truth was, Emily had missed her mother ever since she'd lost her. And Gloria with her kindness and honest observations was someone Emily would like in her life.

Ten minutes later, Emily sat in Jared's sedan beside him as he pulled into the driveway at his home. Courtney had fallen asleep in her car seat and Amy was almost there.

"I can help you get the girls to bed," she offered, not ready to leave him yet, feeling more and more drawn to Amy and Courtney.

"When I bring them home alone and they fall asleep, I have to wake them up. I don't like to leave one of them in the car while I take the other inside."

"I can understand that."

"On the other hand, I don't want you to feel obliged that you have to do anything."

"I don't feel obliged. When we're not at work, Jared, you're not my boss. We're just two people. If you're afraid you're taking advantage of me, you're not. I want to be here."

She felt him studying her in the darkness.

"All right. Let's take them inside."

As Emily carried Amy and Jared carried Courtney, she felt a closeness to him. They didn't seem to need words to establish understanding. It was almost as if words would muddle up the connection they had. Yet Emily knew the time was coming when she'd have to tell him everything about her. That idea scared her.

Emily helped Jared change the girls into their night-clothes, feeling motherly. She liked the feeling. After she pulled Amy's sheet up to her chin, she kissed her on the forehead. It just seemed the natural and right thing to do. Jared did the same with Courtney. Both girls curled on their sides, Courtney with Stardust, Amy with a favorite teddy bear.

Emily and Jared walked down the hall into the great room. There she said, "I'd better go. We both have early days tomorrow."

Jared approached her and rested his hands on her shoulders. "You've been a great help ever since my mom's accident."

"You didn't want me to go along tonight, though, did you?"

"You made the visit easier for Amy and Courtney. But, no, I guess I didn't want you to get more involved in my life."

Her expression must have shown the hurt she felt at his words.

He grimaced. "That didn't come out right."

"I think it did."

"Emily, damn it all," he swore. "Every time I'm near you, I want to kiss you. In the hospital bathroom I wanted to tug you into my arms. Damn it," he said again, his arms enfolding her. "I've wanted to do this all night." He bent his head to hers and kissed her.

Their lips melded together. His tongue invaded her mouth. He was hungry, demanding, possessive. This time, he didn't restrain his need and she responded to it, seeking the strokes of his tongue, kissing him back for all she was worth.

He backed her up to the sofa and they fell onto it, holding on to each other, breaking the kiss and coming back for more.

Emily liked everything about being with Jared. She loved touching him. She loved the feel of her fingers laced in his thick hair. She loved exploring the taut skin at his neck.

Jared groaned and slid his hands under her top. When his thumbs found her nipples and teased them through her bra, she thought she'd explode. She was lost in what they were when they were together like this. But he must have been aware of reality all along…because he let his hands drop away and slip out from under her top.

Moments later he tore his lips from hers and muttered, "We've got to stop."

"Why?" She couldn't believe she asked it, but she needed to know.

He looked sad as he stroked her face and pushed wayward curls from her forehead. "Because we don't want to make a mess of each other's lives."

She opened her eyes and stared into his. "Why are you so sure that would happen?"

"I just am."

"No, I don't think you're sure. You just don't want to open yourself up to the possibility. You've been hurt and you don't want to take the chance that will happen again. I've been hurt, too, Jared. And yes, the possibility of getting hurt again scares me. But I feel a connection to you."

"A connection…or an attraction?" he asked bluntly.

"Both. Don't you feel both?"

"Right now, I only know what my body's telling me. You're a sexy woman and I haven't touched a woman since my marriage ended. That's a pretty powerful driving force. I'm not going to let it drive me to do something we'll both regret."

She pushed herself up from the sofa. "Don't think for me, Jared, and don't make decisions for me. If you want to back off for your own reasons, that's fine. But don't make the mistake of thinking you know what's going on in *my* head." Or in my heart, she added to herself.

He stood now, too, but she didn't want to see the look in his eyes that told her he thought this was all about sex.

She grabbed her purse from the coffee table where she'd dropped it and headed for the door.

"Emily…"

"I'll see you at work tomorrow, Jared. At least there, we know exactly how to treat each other. We know exactly what we have to do."

She left Jared's house, his mother's words echoing in her head. *Don't give up on him if he seems to push you away.*

To do that, she'd have to be more vulnerable than she'd ever been before. She wasn't sure being that vulnerable was a risk she wanted to take.

"I'm going to tell Grady I'm pregnant tonight," Francesca said the next evening. Emily had just walked in the door as her friend was getting ready to go out.

"Where are you meeting him?" Emily asked, assessing Francesca's western-cut tan pantsuit. Her long, straight brown hair curved over her shoulder. She looked fabulous.

"At the saddle shop."

"Alone?"

"Hopefully. This isn't the kind of news I'd want to give him in public. The only thing is—"

"Are you afraid something else will happen?" Emily guessed, and when her friend's cheeks turned red, she knew she'd guessed correctly.

"I don't want a relationship, Emily. I'm not ready for one. And things would never work out between us. We're much too different."

Emily wondered how many times her friend had told herself that and if she was using it as an excuse. Francesca was just downright afraid to get involved with a man again.

Francesca checked her watch. "I should be going, but tell me how things went with you and Jared today. You were upset when you came home last night."

"He was at the hospital most of the day. I didn't see him. Maybe that's good."

"Is it?"

"I don't know. When did life get so complicated?"

Francesca shook her head. "When chemistry turned into more than a science experiment. See you later."

Emily had to smile at her friend's assessment of the situation. She took off her jacket and was about to hang it in the closet when the telephone rang. Crossing to the cordless phone beside the sofa, she picked up the handset and checked the caller ID. It was Jared.

"Hello," she said, not knowing what to expect.

"Emily, it's Jared."

"I know."

"What would we do without caller ID?" he teased lightly. "At least you picked up. That's a good sign."

"A good sign for what?"

The silence on his end almost made her wish she hadn't asked. Then he replied, "I've been thinking about last night. I couldn't get it off my mind all day."

She waited.

"You were right. There is a connection between us and I'm not sure it's one I want."

"That's why you called?"

She heard him blow out a breath. "I'm not doing this very well. Just let me say I'm not calling because I need help with the girls."

"I don't mind helping you, Jared."

"I know. But now I'd like to do something that doesn't involve them."

Was he going to ask her on a date? "Like what?"

"There's a charity banquet and dance at the Rayburn Hotel on Saturday evening."

"Yes, I know. I was planning to go with friends."

"How would you like to go with me instead?"

Actually, she'd been planning to tag along with Vince and Tessa.

"Would your friends mind if you changed your plans?" he cut in before she could think it through.

"No, I don't suppose they would. I'd been planning to sit with Tessa Rossi and her husband, Vince. Maybe the four of us could share a table, unless you had something else in mind."

"No, I didn't."

"If you'd rather sit with Dr. Pratt or Dr. Layman…" Those were the two men who shared Jared's practice.

"Larry Pratt isn't going, and Tom is sitting with the hospital board. The thing is, Emily, I'm not asking you because this is a hospital function."

"Why are you asking me?" she inquired softly, not wanting to put him on the spot but needing to know.

"I'd like to spend some time with you alone, away from my daughters, away from the practice. I realized—" He stopped. "I realized what I said last night might have hurt you, and I never meant to do that. Although it's no excuse, I haven't had a personal life for a long time."

"So this is a date?"

"Yes, it's a date. Are you accepting?"

"I'm accepting."

"Good."

She thought she could hear a smile in his voice. Thank goodness she had the rest of the week to think about what to wear. She might have to go shopping!

"That's settled, then. Dinner starts at eight. I'll pick you up around seven fifteen. Is that okay?"

"That's fine."

"I'm glad you're going with me, Emily. I really mean that."

"I'm glad I'm going, too."

After he said good-bye and hung up, Emily couldn't keep from smiling. In fact, she felt like singing. She was definitely going to wait up for Francesca tonight and tell her her news.

Francesca knocked at the door of the saddle shop, her palms sweating. Grady had told her to come around back and park there in the small lot. It was well-lit. She wasn't afraid of getting mugged.

What was she afraid of?

Seeing Grady again? Feeling the attraction that had tumbled them into intimacy? Here was where it had happened—in his office on the blue-denim couch.

Pushing the images out of her head, she knocked sharply on the door again. There was a dim light inside, a brighter one to the right…in his office.

He opened the door and one look into his deep blue eyes told her he, too, was remembering everything that had happened here. He had coal-black hair that she had run her fingers through. He had broad shoulders that had felt so muscled under her hands. He had a stubbled jaw and that stubble had felt—

"Come on in," he invited her with a Texas drawl that should have seemed ordinary, but wasn't.

Her mouth went as dry as the west Texas dirt.

She followed him inside, inhaling the scents of leather, wood, other materials he used for his custom-made saddles. She didn't pay any attention to the worktables, the bench that Grady had told her his dad had handcrafted for him. Rather she followed Grady into that small lit room.

He went behind his desk and sat in the high-back chair. She didn't sit in one of the chairs in front of the desk. Instead she stayed standing. "I won't take up much of your time."

He leaned back, making the chair squeak. "Take all the time you want. I'm not really thrilled with returning to the bookwork program on my computer."

To Grady's right, a cursor blinked on a ledgerlike screen.

There was no point in making small talk. That wasn't why she had come. "I'm pregnant."

The two words hung suspended in the air between them.

"Are you saying the baby's mine?"

She had never imagined he'd doubt that when she told him. "Of course the baby's yours. You're the only man I've slept with in a year. But if you don't believe me, then we don't have anything to talk about." She turned, ready to leave, almost eager to leave.

But Grady shot out of his desk chair, was around his desk, and grabbing her elbow. "Hold on there. It was just a question."

Gazing into his eyes, she realized it was a question he'd had to ask. After all, they didn't know each other.

"We used a condom," she said lamely, knowing that form of contraception was usually reliable but not foolproof.

Grady sighed and rubbed his hand across his forehead. "Yes, we did, but it was a condom I've had in my wallet for a while."

"It could have broken?"

"Possibly. Or you could have gotten pregnant before I put it on."

She felt heat crawl into her cheeks. There had been foreplay—teasing foreplay as she'd never experienced before.

Completely aware of his hand on her arm, the tingles dancing up and down, she pulled out of his grasp and had to make something clear. "I don't want anything from you, Grady. We'd already decided seeing each other again would be a mistake. This doesn't change that."

"The heck it doesn't." His drawl had become more pronounced with each word. "I'm going to want a DNA test after the baby's born."

Her heart lurched. She did *not* want a relationship, especially not with a man who couldn't trust. The idea of getting involved again, getting penned up, trapped, controlled, almost made her panic.

He must have seen the look in her eye because he asked, "What's wrong?"

"I'm going to have this child and raise this child and love this child. But that doesn't mean you and I have to be…connected."

"What has you so spooked? You weren't like this that night."

No, she wasn't. That night had been full of wonder and impulse. When she'd met Grady, the chemistry between them had been so strong she hadn't thought about the next day or a week from that night.

"I'm not spooked. I just don't want to be involved."

"You *are* spooked. You're afraid I'll do something you don't want me to do. So why did you tell me?"

"You had the right to know. Sagebrush is a small town."

"And I could put have two and two together easily if I saw you pregnant and figured out the dates."

"Yes," she admitted, wanting to turn from his probing blue eyes but unable to do so.

His voice lowered…was gentle yet more intense. "You're *not* going to cut me out of the baby's life. If I'm a dad, I'm going be a dad. Do you understand that, Francesca?"

She went cold inside from the thought of him wanting any kind of control, and licked her dry lips. "What does that mean?"

"It means I want to spend time with my son or daughter. I want to have a say in decisions. I want to act like a real parent. I've looked forward all my life to being a dad. I'm not going to let the opportunity slip away."

Grady came from a large family, a loving family, and she should have realized he'd feel this way.

"Don't look so scared, Frannie. I'm not going to try to take custody away from you, if that's what you're thinking."

She didn't know what she was thinking. No one had ever called her Frannie.

"I'm not scared," she returned defensively, squaring her shoulders. "I'm just worried you'll want to tell me what to do and that's not going to happen."

He eyed her assessingly. "I guess we really don't

know each other, do we? One night on the sofa doesn't a couple make."

"No, it doesn't. And we're *not* a couple."

He let a few pounding heartbeats pass before he asked, "When are you due?"

"February twenty-seventh."

"What are you going to do about your practice?"

"I haven't figured everything out yet. I've only known a short while."

He cocked his head. "Did you think about not telling me and moving away from Sagebrush?"

She was hoping her guilt didn't show.

"You did, didn't you?" he accused. Then calmly he asked, "What made you decide to stay and not run?"

"I'm not a coward. I have a life here. I'm not going to let any man make me give up what I'm building."

He slid his hands into the back pockets of his jeans—as if maybe he wanted to do something else with them—and continued to study her. "So what do you suggest we do?"

"I'd like you to give me time—the length of my pregnancy—to figure some things out."

A line creased his brow and he didn't seem to like the idea. Yet he asked, "You'll call me when the baby's born?"

She nodded.

His strong jaw set and his mouth formed a tight line. "I have one condition."

"What?"

"You e-mail me a report every time you go to the doctor just to let me know everything's okay."

For some reason, she didn't quibble. She didn't see the condition as manipulation. Grady was asking her to communicate with him and it didn't have to be in a personal way, just in the form of a report. She could do that.

"All right," she agreed. "That won't be a problem."

"Have you been to see a doctor yet?" he asked.

"Yes, yesterday. Dr. Jared Madison's my doctor. Every other month, I'll see his obstetrical nurse practitioner. She's my roommate, Emily Diaz. When I hit the third trimester, I'll see him."

Grady reached over to his desk and picked up a card from the holder there. He turned it around and jotted something on the back. Then he handed it to her. "My e-mail address is on the front. My cell phone number's on the back. If you need anything—"

"I won't, Grady. Really."

"When you go into labor, I want to know."

"When I go into labor? Why?"

"Because I want to be with you. I want to anticipate this baby being born and be there when he or she is. I mean it, Frannie. Don't deny me that right."

Remembering the night they'd spent together—his passion, tenderness and hunger, she assured him, "I won't," controlling her voice so it wouldn't tremble. Then she tucked his card into her purse and turned to leave.

He followed her to the door.

After he'd opened it for her, he suggested, "I want you to think about the benefit of a child having two parents rather than one. I know it won't be easy to do, but we're smart people. We should be able to figure it out."

She'd have six and a half more months to figure this out, thank goodness. She had a feeling she was going to need every day of those six and a half months to decide how she could coparent with Grady without being involved with him. Getting involved when she was actually ready for it wouldn't be easy. Getting involved in this situation would be sheer lunacy.

As she said good-bye and left, she realized she liked having a nickname for the first time in her life…and she liked the sound of that nickname on Grady Fitzgerald's lips.

Chapter Seven

Emily was concerned Jared had changed his mind about wanting to be with her at the charity banquet. He'd been quiet ever since he picked her up Saturday evening.

Now as they stood outside the ballroom, he asked, "Would you like me to check your shawl?"

"Please," she replied, not wanting to be encumbered by the wrap at the dinner table.

She'd begun to shrug it off when she felt Jared's large hand at her shoulder, helping her remove it. As his fingers brushed against her collarbone, she trembled. She glanced at him over her shoulder. When he gazed into her eyes, they seemed frozen in time. She was sure she saw desire in his eyes, but she wasn't sure what else.

"Jared, is something wrong tonight?" she asked softly.

He let out a long sigh. "You mean besides the fact that you look prettier than I've ever seen you?"

There was frustration in his voice as his eyes ran over the black silk-jersey halter dress with its cranberry trim around the decolletage and hem. She'd worn her hair swept up into a bed of curls, and garnets dangled from delicate gold chain earrings.

His compliment bathed her with its male appreciation and she didn't understand the problem.

Loose curls from her upswept hairdo dangled around her face. He fingered one and wrapped it around his index finger. "When you opened your door to me tonight, I didn't want to bring you to some charity dinner. I wanted to—"

"Emily! Jared! We've been waiting for you. We snatched one of the tables for four." Tessa rushed up to them and gave Emily a hug. "It seems like forever since I've seen you."

Emily hugged her friend back. She missed Tessa's presence in the house, but she wanted Jared to finish that sentence. She wanted to hear what he felt.

Tessa's husband, Vince, gave her a hug, too. In the past month, she'd gotten to know him better and considered him a friend. She introduced him to Jared and the men shook hands.

"You were the chief of police in Sagebrush for a while, weren't you?" Jared asked Vince.

"For a few months. I just started working for an investigative and security firm in Lubbock."

Tessa hooked her arm through her husband's. "We'd better reclaim our table or somebody might steal it."

After Jared checked Emily's shawl, his hand moved to the small of her back. She could feel the imprint of it through the thin fabric. "We'll talk later," he mumbled, guiding her into the ballroom.

Emily saw many faces she recognized. But with Jared's

hand on her back, her mind focused on his hand's heat and texture and the trill of sparks that skipped down her spine. There was always heat when the two of them were together. What *had* he been about to say? That he wanted to make love to her? That he would rather have closed the door at her house and spent the night in bed with her? Could she satisfy him? Would his desire last beyond one night?

At the table, he pulled out her chair for her. When she sat, he leaned close as he pushed her in. If she turned her head, her cheek might graze his jaw. She took in a deep breath.

Jared straightened, but she was still so aware of him. The current between them tonight was lightning hot, lightning fast, and as dangerous as lightning.

Jared took the seat around the corner from Emily. She noticed the way his dark-brown hair waved over his forehead, the way his brow creased as if he was deep in thought. He was wearing a charcoal suit and a red-and-charcoal tie tonight. She saw him in a suit practically every day, but tonight—he seemed bigger than life, more than her boss, more than a friend. Maybe she was just deluding herself, believing he might be falling for her, too.

"Emily tells me she's been spending time with your daughters," Tessa observed, glancing from Emily to Jared as if she could sense the current rippling between them.

"Yes, she has," Jared replied. "She's very good with them."

Tessa smiled fondly at Emily. "She's one of our favorite babysitters."

"How old are your children?" Jared asked.

Emily was grateful he was keeping the conversation going.

Tessa let Vince answer. "Natalie is fourteen months. Sean is ten months. You should bring the girls over sometime. The four of them would probably have a great play session."

Emily watched Jared to see if he was open to the suggestion. To her surprise, he said, "That would be great. Amy and Courtney go to preschool now, but that's only for three days a week."

"What about tomorrow?" Tessa asked. "We can try out our new grill. Are you free?" she asked Emily.

Emily felt awkward. She didn't want Jared to feel forced to spend time with her. She wasn't sure what to say. "Yes, I'm free, but—" She glanced at Jared. "You three have a lot in common with your kids. I don't want you to feel as if you have to invite me…." She trailed off.

Tessa looked from Emily to Jared. "I'm not playing matchmaker. I just thought we might all have a good time."

Jared stepped into the awkwardness and covered Emily's hand with his. Tingles swept up her arm. "I enjoy Emily's company and I'm sure with four kids around we can use her help keeping them on an even keel."

A three-piece band had been setting up and as they began playing couples headed to the dance floor.

Jared asked Emily, "Would you like to dance?"

"It's been so long since I've been on a dance floor, I don't know if I remember how."

"It's like riding a bicycle," he teased, stood and offered her his hand. She took it, rising to her feet. With her hand in Jared's, she felt…excited but safe. Her breaths quickened as she anticipated being held in his arms once more.

On the dance floor, they stood in the ballroom dancing position, a good six inches apart. Then he gave her a crooked smile, pulled her a little closer and wrapped his fingers tighter around hers.

Her breasts against his chest, her cheek against the fabric of his suit, she inhaled his cologne and felt almost dizzy from just being so close.

After the first verse of the song, Jared asked, "Why would you think I wouldn't want you to go with me to Tessa and Vince's?"

"Do you?" she asked, holding her breath.

"Yes." His fingers moved against hers. "But it's much safer for us to be in a crowd like this, or to be with another couple with kids around."

Safer.

Now his eyes were serious. "I don't want to hurt you. I told you I don't want to get involved with anyone again. I never intend to remarry. Once was enough."

He was so certain. Her hopes for more than one night, for a committed relationship dissolved. Yet maybe if she told him how *she* felt... "You and I both came through a divorce, but I guess I feel differently about it. I'd like to have a second chance at finding real happiness."

"I'd rather just be content."

She couldn't argue with him about that, but she wanted more than contentment. She wanted to share her life, share her thoughts, share her dreams. But Jared didn't. He was making himself perfectly clear.

For a short while, they simply danced. Jared's firm guidance made it easy, though her heart raced at the slide of his fingers down her back, the pressure of his palm against hers. The expression on his face told her serious passion could develop between them if he let it.

Would he let it? Would she?

One song segued into the next and the dance floor became more crowded. Jared brought Emily closer to him. When she looked up, her lips were very near his cheek. The nerve in his jaw worked and she thought she could feel the thumping of his heart. Maybe the sensation was hers pounding even harder.

"You wanted to know why I was so quiet tonight when I picked you up." His voice was low…intimate.

"I wondered if you regretted asking me to come tonight."

Leaning back slightly, he studied her, then shook his head. "Your ex-husband must have done a number on you. Any man would be glad to escort you."

She felt herself blushing.

"You're part of the reason why I was quiet. It's not because I don't want to be with you, because I do."

"What's the other part?"

"My mind's on a discussion I had with my mother this afternoon."

"She's in rehab now?"

"Yes. And she's making progress. But she's worried. She's worried she'll be a burden rather than an asset when she comes home. She's thinking that maybe after rehab, she should go into an assisted-living facility."

"But you don't think she should."

"Only if that's what she really wants. I think she's just frustrated with not recovering more quickly, and after another week or so, she'll be stronger. I also think she'll be happier if she lives with us. If she can't take care of the girls, I'll hire a nanny. But I think it's better for her to be with us than to be alone in a tiny apartment."

"No one wants to be a burden."

"I understand that."

Emily gazed into his troubled green eyes. "There's something else going on, isn't there? This isn't about just her ability to take care of the girls."

He was slow to respond, but finally said, "She doesn't believe I really want her around. We haven't had the best relationship over the years."

Suspecting she was stepping into very deep water, Emily asked, "*Do* you want her around?"

Now he went silent altogether.

"I shouldn't have asked. Your family is none of my business." She knew Jared's privacy was important to him. She shouldn't have probed.

Their bodies were still close, the attraction between them as strong as ever. But Jared's restraint was palpable and so was his intent. He was *not* going to get seriously involved with her, definitely not emotionally, and maybe not even physically.

This time after a sixties' ballad ended, they went back to the table, the tension between them obvious. The strain between them was such a contrast to the loving devotion between Vince and Tessa. Emily knew that devotion had started in high school. They'd undergone heartache and a long separation until they'd found each other again.

Emily wondered if she yearned to jump into a relationship with Jared because she was beginning to care for his girls. Maybe she just basically wanted to be a mom.

But then she looked over at him, their gazes locked, her heart lurched, attraction pulsed between them. She knew her growing feelings for Jared were altogether separate from her affection for his daughters.

Over dinner, Vince and Jared talked about security problems in businesses. Tessa and Jared spoke in general of their practices. Emily and Jared seemed to have nothing to say to each other. Because he didn't want to let her in? Because she wanted too much? Could they settle for friendship?

At the end of the evening, after goodbyes and "see you tomorrow" to Tessa and Vince, Emily and Jared walked to his car. The silence between them was so strained that she wished she had driven herself.

Jared tried to make small talk in the car on the way home. "Dinner was good for a group that size."

"Yes, it was," she agreed, although the prime rib had tasted like sawdust in her mouth.

Taking the cue, she made a stab at small talk, too. "Did Vince tell you they're building a barn on their property? They want to adopt wild mustangs and gentle them."

"Yes, he told me about that. He mentioned Tessa's father is involved."

"At one time, Tessa's dad and Vince butted heads. Her dad didn't approve of Vince twenty years ago. It's nice to see they're becoming friends now."

Jared went quiet again, and she realized she'd probably said the wrong thing. Parents and children reuniting, reconciling, resolving their differences wasn't something he wanted to talk about.

Suddenly Emily's phone rang. It was Francesca. "Hi, what's up?" Emily asked.

"I just wanted you to know I'm at the hospital and I'll be tied up for a few more hours. I didn't want you to worry. How was dinner?"

"We're on our way home."

"That didn't answer my question."

"No, I guess it didn't."

"Uh-oh. That bad, huh?"

"Possibly."

"All right. I'll get the scoop in the morning."

"Thanks for letting me know." Emily closed her phone.

"A problem?" Jared asked.

"No. Francesca's going to be tied up at the hospital for a while. She didn't want me to worry."

"Women are very different from men," he remarked.

"How so?"

"You've only known Francesca and Tessa for what? About eight months?"

"That's right."

"Yet your friends act as if you've been friends for years."

"We clicked when we met. We seemed to understand each other instantly. Yet we didn't trust right away. That came slowly." It had only been this summer that she'd told Francesca and Tessa about her career as a midwife and everything that had happened.

"Relationships are all about trust, aren't they?" he mused, and she wondered what he meant by that. It sounded as if trust was an issue for him, too. Because of his marriage? Or more precisely, his divorce? Would he ever tell her about that?

Fifteen minutes later, Jared pulled into the driveway that led to the detached garage beside the old Victorian. "You *do* have a thoughtful roommate. She left the light on for you."

The Tiffany light in the foyer cast its jeweled glow behind the sheer curtains, making the house appear welcoming.

Emily opened her clutch purse and took out her keys. "You don't have to walk me to the door. I'll be fine."

If she just hopped out, said good-bye here, they wouldn't have the awkwardness, the question to kiss or not to kiss.

But Jared shook his head and unlatched his seat belt. "I know you'll be fine, but I'm going to walk you to the door anyway."

Then he was out of the car and coming around to the passenger side. He opened her door and offered her his hand to help her out.

She told herself he was simply being a gentleman. Chivalry wasn't dead. But it didn't have to mean any more than a man being polite to his date.

They walked up the curved cement pathway, not touching, not talking, looking straight ahead instead of glancing at each other. The streetlamp shed enough light that Emily could see to insert her key into the lock. She was aware of Jared behind her on the small, flagstone stoop as she pushed the door open. She planned to just say good-night.

But Jared surprised her by asking, "Do you mind if I come in?"

Now she *did* look at him. "I don't mind."

Jared followed her inside, then slowly closed the door. "Tonight didn't go the way I'd planned," he admitted.

"I know. I thought we'd just have a relaxed evening and enjoy each other's company."

He took a step closer to her. The multicolor tones of the lamp created an intimate atmosphere as he rested his hands on her shoulders. "I'm anything but relaxed when I'm with you."

They were both breathing faster…both waiting for whatever happened next. Maybe he was giving her the chance to back up or turn away. She wasn't going to do that. Already her feelings for him were too serious to deny.

Without further warning, he embraced her. His mouth covered hers in a demanding kiss that took her breath away. Responding to Jared was as instinctive as breathing. He groaned as she reached around his neck and laced her hands in his hair. Warning bells in her head demanded she be careful. She knew this desire they were giving into was dangerous. Yet hadn't she wanted this all night? They were alone now. Hadn't she dreamed about intimacy with Jared that went beyond stolen kisses?

He broke the embrace to separate the edges of her shawl. Afterward, he pushed it over her shoulders. It fell to the floor. Free now, unencumbered by the layer of fabric, she tunneled her hands under his suit jacket, wrapped her arms around him and felt his heat through his shirt. He was still for a few moments as if he were appreciating that type of intimacy. But then, ready for more, he broke away to shrug off his jacket. It fell to the floor on top of her shawl.

Touching became as high a priority as kissing. He passed his hands up and down her bare arms, then removed the pins that held the curls on top of her head. One by one, they pinged as they landed on the hardwood floor. In no time, her hair was down around her face and he was stroking his fingers through it, angling her head so he could kiss her deeply, so his tongue could explore more thoroughly, so they could fall more overwhelmingly into their desire. Jared wasn't seducing her. This wasn't about seduction. It was about mutual need. She needed Jared. She was falling in love with him. She needed to know he wanted her as much as she wanted him. His hungry, fevered kisses told her that he did. His touch reiterated the same hunger.

When Jared fingered the fastener at the back of her neck, he hesitated for an instant and she knew why. He was giving her the opportunity to say stop. He was giving her a few moments to decide if she wanted to go further.

She didn't need time to think. Right or wrong, smart or stupid, risky or dangerous didn't matter. Only she and Jared together mattered.

Giving him the go-ahead, she tugged his tie down and began unbuttoning his shirt. Her actions were a clear message he quickly read. He nimbly unhooked the fastener under her hair, then slid down the zipper at the back of her dress. With tantalizing slowness, he let the fabric drop but didn't push it from her breasts. Rather he kissed her collarbone, lingered at her neck, moved an earring aside to tongue the shell of her ear. The tingling sensation on her skin, the intimate brush of his lips was as exciting as his kiss. Shivers danced down her spine and a delicious warmth began curling in her womb. It had been so long since she'd felt desirable…so long since she'd acknowledged her needs as a woman. Those needs included being touched and caressed and kissed. In her marriage, she'd always let Richard lead. Now she felt bold and needed to give pleasure, too, rather than just receive it. She slid her hand inside his shirt and caressed his chest.

Jared mumbled, "Emily, You're going to make this happen too fast."

"What's wrong with that?" she asked, giving him a saucy grin.

With a wide smile, he pushed her dress from her breasts. "You're not wearing a bra."

"The bra's in the dress," she whispered.

"How convenient." Leaning forward, he trailed kisses above each breast, then around them. He was driving her crazy, but she loved it. Finally he slid her dress down her hips and it fell to her feet. She was naked from the waist up, lacy bikini pants below.

With Richard, even after six years of marriage, she'd still felt self-conscious as if her figure were too lush, as if she didn't match his ideal of a perfect woman. But the way Jared was looking at her, she was glad her breasts were full, proud her hips were rounded. She felt no self-consciousness at all and wondered who she was becoming.

"Do you know how sexy you look in your panties and high heels?"

"No," she admitted.

He took a breast into each palm, bent his head and kissed one nipple, then the other. When his tongue teased her there, she thought her knees were going to give way.

He must have guessed because he scooped her up into his arms and carried her into the living room to the sofa. The moon shone through the window, casting just enough light that she could see the intense desire in his eyes.

When he laid her on the sofa, she teased, "Maybe I should see how sexy *you* look in your underwear and shoes."

He laughed, a joyous laugh she'd never heard from him. Then he was kissing her again, undressing her completely.

Suddenly he stopped and seemed frozen.

"What's wrong?"

"I don't have a condom."

She sat up and took his hand. "I'm on birth control…a hormone IUD." She stopped, then went on. "I never had it removed."

She thought Jared would start kissing her again. She thought they'd pick up where they'd left off.

"You're really on birth control?" he asked as if he didn't believe what she'd told him.

All she could do was reassure him. "I really am. But if you're concerned about anything else…"

He seemed to come to some conclusion. "No. Nothing else."

Quickly Jared shucked off his clothes and stretched over her on the sofa. They lay still, appreciating the intimate fit of their bodies the moment before desire plunged ahead into no-return passion. When Jared kissed her neck, she stroked his back, knowing they'd started a dance that could only end in completion.

Emily reached down and caressed Jared. He groaned, accepted the pleasure for a few moments, then took her hand away. "I want to make sure you're ready."

She was stunned by his thoughtfulness. But tonight it wasn't necessary. "I'm ready now."

He took her at her word and propped himself on his elbows. As he kissed her mouth, she thought she'd climax without him being inside her. But that would be such a loss.

He entered her with a long, smooth thrust. Their bodies glistened now and she'd never been hotter, more excited, more aroused. Jared drove into her again and again. All she could do was instinctively wrap her legs around him and hold on tight.

The climax, when it came, was a hailstorm of sensations. Delicious tingles began at her center and spread to every nerve ending. Her body tightened and then wondrously unwound, shaking her until she trembled all over.

Jared went still, waiting for her to enjoy every last wave of pleasure. Then he pressed deeper and harder and faster until she came again and he found a shuddering release.

They lay there in the profound silence. Emily's heart rate slowed as she caught her breath and floated back to earth.

Jared raised his head and asked, "Are you okay?"

A deep concern in his voice tightened her throat. "I'm good. How about you?"

He brushed her hair away from her cheek. "I'd like to tell you that this isn't what I intended when we came in. But…I think subconsciously this is what I wanted since the day I hired you."

"But you didn't *know* me."

"Chemistry like we have has nothing to do with knowing."

"I don't believe that. Are you saying you hired me because you wanted to have sex with me?"

He swore. "I knew I shouldn't have said anything. I knew this was going to get complicated."

"We just had sex, Jared. Sex is complicated, at least for me. I don't have sex with any man I just happen to be attracted to."

"And you're the only woman I've had sex with since my divorce." He pulled away from her and sat up as if that revelation had been a little too honest. "Bathroom?" he asked.

"To the right. Under the stairs."

The night drafts seemed to invade the house, and Emily suddenly felt cold. She was falling in love with Jared Madison. That idea was terrifying enough. But the really scary part was that he would look on tonight as if it were just pure sexual pleasure. Hadn't he felt more than that? Hadn't he felt something that went beyond the physical?

There was an afghan on the back of the sofa and she reached for it, sitting up, and wrapping it around herself.

Jared had picked up his clothes on the way to the bathroom. When he returned to her, he'd flung on his shirt and slacks, but the shirt was still unbuttoned and hung loose. "I'd better go," he said, sitting beside her on the sofa, reaching for his socks.

"We have a bottle of brandy Tessa's father gave her. Or I can make coffee."

"I'd better get home. I'm sure Chloie would rather sleep in her own bed than on my sofa." He slipped into his shoes and tied them.

"Jared—"

Straightening, he settled his arm around her and kissed her lightly on the lips. "I did not mean to suggest I hired you because I wanted to have sex with you. I just meant the first time I saw you, I was attracted to you. More than attracted to you. But I never intended to act on it. Then suddenly, there you were, so gentle and compassionate with my daughters, eager to help. I never wanted to take advantage of you."

"You haven't."

"I'm not sure about that. I do know tonight was a mistake and one we shouldn't repeat."

Deep down, she'd known that's what he was going to say. Giving in to desire had a price. That price could be even thicker walls between them. She hoped not. That was the last thing she wanted.

Jared said, "About tomorrow. What should we do?" He meant about their get-together with Tessa and Vince.

"Do you still want to go?"

Jared considered it. "I'd like to see their place, the barn and what they're doing. It would be good for the girls to spend time with other children."

"I could just not go."

"You suggested that before and I vetoed it, remember? Tessa and Vince are *your* friends. How uncomfortable would you be if we both go?"

"I can focus on the kids and help Tessa in the kitchen. There's no reason why we both can't have a good time."

She wanted to believe that. She didn't want to cut Jared out of her life or have him cut her out of his. She still believed they had a chance for more, if he'd only let his guard down…if he'd only believe he could be happy and have more in his life than his children and his work.

"It's settled," she said with a shrug, as if none of it really mattered, as if sex were just casual entertainment, as if her feelings for Jared hadn't taken on a whole new dimension tonight. "I'll meet you at Tessa and Vince's at four."

When Jared studied her, Emily hoped he was only

seeing her mussed hair, her heated cheeks, her just-kissed lips. She hoped he wasn't seeing the love growing in her heart for him.

If he saw that, he would cut her out of his life.

Last night had shaken Jared to his core.

The scent of sage drifted with the wind as he glanced at the cotton fields in the distance, then watched Amy and Courtney toss a sponge ball to fourteen-month-old Natalie. Emily sat on a blanket with ten-month-old Sean in front of her. With his shoulder still mending after surgery earlier in the summer, he didn't yet have full use of his arm. But Vince had told Jared his son had come a long way.

Jared stood at the edge of the yard where the foundation of the new barn lay waiting for the construction crew.

Tessa strolled toward him, her blond hair blowing in the wind. She was a beautiful woman but…he'd never been attracted to her. So why did Emily pack such a punch? Why could she turn him on with a lift of her brow, a smile, a look?

"Don't you love to watch them play?" she asked Jared.

"I do. I really love to hear them laugh."

"I know. Laughter means everything is right in their world."

"I think about when Amy and Courtney grow up. If they'll still be close…if they'll go to the same colleges."

Amy ran over to Emily, dropped the ball into Sean's lap, then laid her head on Emily's shoulder.

"Your twins like Emily."

"They do."

Tessa didn't say anything for a few moments, but he could tell she had something on her mind. He waited.

Finally she looked away from the kids to him. "Emily's still vulnerable."

"Meaning?" He didn't like anyone poking into his life, but he knew Tessa meant well.

Last night you and Emily seemed…closer than boss and employee. Today you're staying a room apart. I know this is your business and hers, but she's a good friend, Jared. I want to see her happy. Not hurt again. When she first moved to Sagebrush—" Tessa stopped and her expression said she might have revealed too much.

All Jared had to do was think about the way Emily had given herself to him last night. She'd been free, passionate, erotically sensual. He'd even trusted her word she was on birth control. And he didn't trust women easily anymore.

"Her husband was a bastard, wasn't he? She hasn't said much. But I've gotten the feeling she felt used…put down."

He could see Tessa didn't know whether to answer or not. Finally she replied, "I think you're on the mark."

After last night, Jared knew Emily deserved a man who wasn't closed off to her…a man who trusted wholeheartedly and could dream. He was closed off. He didn't dream anymore except for a happy future for his twins. He wasn't the man for her.

He assured Tessa, "I won't hurt Emily." He knew he wouldn't because he was going to keep his distance. They would work together amicably and he would shut down his desire for her. He could do it.

He'd had a lot of practice shutting down and burying his feelings ever since he was ten. It shouldn't be hard to do now.

Chapter Eight

Emily was falling in love with a man who didn't want to love! She couldn't stop thinking about the passionate sex she'd shared with Jared, his polite-bordering-on-cool attitude at Tessa's and the icy wall he'd erected between them ever since.

She hurried down the cereal aisle of the grocery store after work on Monday, her thoughts focused on the way they'd ignored each other for over a week. As they'd consulted on patients, they'd kept their meetings professional. Yet she'd caught Jared's assessing glances when he thought she wasn't looking, and she'd had a difficult time thinking about him simply as her boss.

Ahead of Emily, farther down the long aisle, a young woman crouched down to her cart. At first Emily thought she might be tucking a large box of cereal underneath. But then Emily realized the woman was pregnant and there was a wet spot near the woman's feet. This young mother-to-be didn't have a box in her hands. She was holding on to the cart for support!

That cart would tip over if she wasn't careful.

Emily rushed to the mother-to-be and knelt beside her. "Are you all right?"

The pretty blond shook her head, sweat beading on her brow. "I'm having contractions. They started early this morning but were just like twinges. I didn't even know they were contractions, so I didn't pay much attention." She held her tummy and grabbed the cart in a strangling grip.

Emily's fingers went to the pregnant woman's wrist as she reflexively took her pulse. "What's your name?"

"Patti. Patti Holbrook." She let go of the cart and took a deep breath.

"How far along are you?" Emily asked.

"Thirty-five weeks."

Emily slipped her cell phone from her purse. "Is there anyone I can call for you?"

Patti shook her head as she grabbed for the cart again to try to pull herself up.

Emily encircled her with her arms. "Come on. Let me help you."

They had almost made it to a standing position when another contraction caused Patti to double over again. She let out a moan.

Emily suspected she might have to do more than drive Patti to the hospital.

One of the elderly gentlemen stocking shelves spotted them and his eyebrows quirked up.

Emily asked him, "Could you please block off this aisle?"

After an assessing look at both of them, he dragged their carts toward the front of the store.

"The pain feels like it's tearing me apart," Patti said tearfully. "I can't have my baby here."

Emily kept her arm around the young woman who looked to be in her late teens.

The stock clerk came hurrying back. "The aisle's blocked. The manager called 911. What else can I do?"

"Can you get me some supplies? The paramedics might not arrive in time, so we need to be ready in case they don't."

"What do you need?"

"Towels and something to cover the floor. A bucket or basin of hot water. Antibacterial soap."

From all the deliveries Emily had attended, she knew what was most important—she had to remain calm.

Patti's contractions began again and she grabbed Emily's arm. Another, much younger man ran up to them with an armful of supplies—a package of plastic sheeting, terry cloth and paper towels. A few moments later the older man returned with the bucket and soap.

Both the manager and the clerk helped Emily spread the plastic sheeting. Patti slid on top of it, looking fearfully up at Emily. "I thought I'd be in a hospital."

Emily shrugged off the jacket to her sundress, folded it and slipped it under Patti's head. "A baby can be delivered anywhere. You'll be fine. I'm going to call the doctor I work with. He might only be a few minutes away. Just hold on."

Taking her phone in hand, Emily speed-dialed Jared's cell phone number. He answered on the first ring.

"Jared, where are you?"

"I just got to the office. I had two deliveries this afternoon. Why?"

"I need you to come to Fresh Food Grocery on High Rock Road. A woman's having a baby."

As Patti clenched her fists and bit her lip, Emily knew

another contraction had begun. She glanced at her watch. "Her contractions are two minutes apart."

He didn't hesitate. "I'm on my way."

Emily moved farther down Patti's side. Jared was on his way. For some reason, just that thought gave her the confidence she needed.

As soon as the contraction ebbed, Emily covered Patti with a towel and helped her undress from the waist down.

"Is he coming?" Patti asked shakily.

"Yes, he is. But if he doesn't arrive in time, it will be okay. I'm a midwife."

"An honest-to-goodness midwife?" The last syllable came out on a squeak and Emily could see Patti was trying not to scream. She said, "I have to push. I really have to push."

As Emily examined Patti, she could see the top of the baby's head.

"Easy now," Emily encouraged her. "You're going to be okay. Take slow deep breaths." She pulled the bucket closer and unwrapped the soap, then scrubbed up to her elbows.

With the baby's head crowning, Emily knew she didn't have much time. She saw Patti tensing up for another contraction.

"Did you take childbirth classes?" she asked Patti.

Patti nodded.

"Okay. Then you know how to breathe. I want you to focus on that box of cereal over there. The one with the bright-blue letters. Keep your attention on it and blow air out while you push."

Patti blew and pushed.

As the baby's head emerged, Emily applied gentle pressure to control the speed of birth, to help prevent damage, both to the baby and the mom. As all of her training rushed back, she made sure the umbilical cord wasn't wrapped around the baby's neck.

"Clean towel!" she called, and the manager pushed it into her hand.

"One more push," she told Patti. "Come on now. A great big push!"

Her heart beating double time, a lump in her throat, Emily carefully supported the baby as its shoulders slid out. Tears burned Emily's eyes as she finally held a baby girl in her hands.

She was barely aware of someone coming up behind her. All of her focus was on the child who wasn't yet breathing! Emily flicked the soles of her feet and rubbed her back. The little girl took a breath, letting out a cry.

Emily wanted to just soak in the wonderful joy of holding a miracle in her hands, but there wasn't time for that. She had to keep the infant warm. She wrapped her in the towel and placed her on Patti's belly as sirens wailed in the distance.

Emily felt a hand on her shoulder. "You did a wonderful job. Maybe I should take over now."

Jared. He had watched her as the baby arrived. She should say the words right now…tell him she was a midwife and she knew what she was doing. The placenta had to be handled carefully. Patti's belly needed to be massaged.

Jared had already rolled up his shirtsleeves and was washing up.

A gaggle of voices at the end of the aisle grew louder. "Make room," she heard someone shout. The paramedics were coming.

Making a quick decision about what was best for Patti, Emily let Jared take over. She stood to the side as she watched him finish the birthing process.

Not long after, the paramedics transferred Patti to a gurney and wheeled her out of the store.

* * *

Jared stood at the door of the grocery store with Emily as the ambulance pulled away. "You did a great job with that delivery."

As he turned to look at her, she knew the moment was now. "Jared, I'm a midwife."

His expression went from confusion to astonishment to something she couldn't read. His voice took on a tense edge. "You're a midwife? And that's a qualification you didn't feel you should put on your résumé?"

She couldn't get defensive…she couldn't. She was in the wrong for not confiding in him. "Are you being my boss now or a…friend?"

He weighed the question, then rubbed his hand up and down the back of his neck. "I don't know if I can separate them. Why would you hide your real profession? You must have had a reason. Is everything else on your résumé true?"

"It's true. I just didn't tell you everything."

A local TV-station van, satellite on top, pulled up in front of the store.

Jared took a long breath and then checked his watch.

A car honked in the parking lot, another slowed and veered close to the curb in front of the store to let out a passenger. The sliding glass doors behind them opened and shut and a middle-aged man pushed his grocery cart to his car.

"You picked a heck of a place to start this discussion," Jared muttered. "And I imagine that news van is here because of what just happened in the store. We don't want to get tied up with them."

Emily had spotted one or two patrons in the store with camera cell phones aimed at the gurney. How much had been recorded?

Jared continued. "I have to get home. Chloie needs to leave by seven. We do need to talk about this, Emily. But not right now."

Two men spilled out of the van, one with video equipment, and ran into the store.

"At your office tomorrow?" Emily asked, uncertain about what to say and where to say it.

As Jared focused his attention on her, she could almost see him remembering the intimate moments they'd shared. Had they meant anything to him? Anything at all?

His green eyes were piercing, and he studied her as if he didn't know her. "Come over to the house about nine thirty. The girls will be in bed and we can talk. I've got to get going."

She watched Jared hurry across the parking lot, climb into his car and drive away.

She had kept the truth from him and now...

Now she might lose her job.

Would she lose her bonds with Jared, too?

Emily rang Jared's doorbell, uncertainty and anxiety dampening her palms.

When Jared opened his door to her, he looked wary. He didn't say anything but moved aside to let her in. He'd changed from his suit into a T-shirt, jeans and boots. Chest hair swirled at the V-neck of his shirt. She wanted to dive into his arms, tell him she was the same person she was yesterday...that nothing had really changed.

Yet something had. She could see it in his eyes. There was mistrust there.

He led her to the sofa. "The girls have been in bed for an hour. The last time I checked, they'd fallen asleep."

She wanted to say something but was waiting for a

signal from him. Instead of taking the chair across from the sofa, he sat down next to her. That gave her some hope.

He wasn't close enough to touch, though, and he sounded very bosslike as he requested, "Tell me what you omitted from your résumé."

Her chest tightened. She wanted him to understand all of it. "Can I start at the beginning?"

"I'm listening."

She hoped he was listening with his heart as well as his head. "I was still in training to become an RN when I decided to become an obstetrical nurse practitioner. I loved taking care of babies and pregnant moms and I assisted at births, volunteered at the free clinic and also did home health care for pregnant mothers. I had lots of conversations with the mothers…with women who wanted to deliver their babies at home. Some were too poor to afford hospital bills without insurance. Some were simply afraid of everything medical. Others wanted an organic birth that was as stress free as it could be. So I went for midwifery training and became certified. For two years afterward, I assisted another midwife. Then I went out on my own."

His gaze was probing as he asked, "Some obstetricians are vehemently opposed to home births. Is that why you didn't want to admit you were a midwife? You thought our practice wouldn't hire you?"

If only that was the reason. If only—

"No. Something happened." She hesitated then began. Now she wanted to have her story out. She just wanted to get it over with.

"I only took on low-risk pregnancies, women who didn't have histories that could cause a problem during labor and delivery. I had an obstetrician to back me up. In all the deliveries I attended, I only had one labor where I sent the mother to the hospital, and she had a C-section. The mom and baby were fine. But then a year later, I attended the delivery of a young, healthy, strong mom with nothing in her history to predict a problem. The dad coached and was involved all the way. But when I delivered their baby, he was stillborn."

Jared didn't speak, so she went on. "The Wilsons were devastated and wanted someone to blame. They filed a complaint and my license was suspended during the investigation. They weren't satisfied with that and also filed a civil lawsuit. I didn't have malpractice insurance. It's simply unaffordable for nurse midwives who deliver at home."

His face unreadable, Jared asked, "What was the result of the lawsuit?"

"The jury decided there was no malpractice."

"An autopsy was performed?"

"It didn't show the cause of death."

"What happened with the licensing board?"

"They also decided there was no malpractice and I retained my license. But the Wilsons had hired a shark of a lawyer. He brought up the C-section birth and said I'd missed something there, too. I doubted myself. What if I had missed something in both cases?"

When she finished, he was silent. So she addressed his original question. "I didn't include my midwifery in my résumé because any time a professional is brought before the board, a cloud hangs over her head. I knew I had that cloud hanging over me and on top of that there was the lawsuit. But even more than that, I can never forget the day the baby was born dead. I lost all my confidence. The look in that young couple's eyes—" Her throat closed and she felt tears start to run.

The room was quiet again. Finally, Jared asked, "If you

had delivered that baby in a hospital and it had been still-born, what would you have felt?"

She took a deep breath and really considered his question. "I would still wonder if there had been something I could have done differently."

"And after you worked for me a few weeks, a few months, you still decided to keep this secret so I wouldn't fire you?"

She understood what he was getting at. She hadn't trusted him. That seemed to bother him even more than the fact that she was a midwife! "Secrets are complicated. Aren't there things about your life you haven't told me?"

"That's very different, Emily. A private life is one thing. A professional life is another."

"Maybe so, but I don't think you're upset with me because I'm a midwife. You're upset with me because I didn't trust you."

He frowned, the lines around his eyes cutting deep. "Our relationship is a mixture of personal and professional, no matter how hard we try to separate them. But I'm going to have to tell my partners about this. They should know."

Jared was a man of integrity and she'd expected as much. "I was right about my job being in jeopardy, wasn't I?"

"If you had just told me—"

She had torn the thread of trust between them. Could Jared forgive her for that? Couldn't he understand how much this job meant to her? How much *he* meant to her?

His phone rang, cutting through the tension. He moved to the end of the sofa to check the caller ID on the handset there. "I don't recognize the number. I'm going to let the machine take it."

They waited until the phone rang two more times and

then a male voice asked, "Dr. Madison? This is Jonus Wingate. I'm a reporter with the *Lubbock Sentinel*. The paramedics gave me your name. I'm writing an article about the birth in the grocery store today and I'd like your input. Please call me as soon as you can. My story will appear in tomorrow afternoon's paper." The reporter left a number.

"The paramedics didn't know who I was," Emily murmured.

"That's a good thing," Jared said wryly. "Don't worry, I'm not calling him back." He ran his hand through his hair and gave her another penetrating look. "Is this all of it? Have you told me everything? Or could this reporter dig up anything else if he learns your name?"

"The reporter won't find anything else. But—"

"But?"

She didn't want *any* secrets between them.

"My marriage was involved in all of this, too. We used a withdrawal from Richard's pension for legal fees. He was trying to get a promotion and he didn't want the publicity. I just wanted him to stand by me and tell me everything would be okay. After it was all over, he said I'd changed, that I wasn't the woman he married. I suppose that was true. I felt like…I lost everything. That's why I moved here to start fresh. I just wanted to pay him back what I owed him and forget about all of it."

"You're paying him back for the legal fees?"

"Every month. It will take a while, but I'm going to do it."

After a few moments of silence, Jared said, "I can understand wanting to move someplace new and start fresh." The depth to his voice led Emily to believe he really *did* understand.

But then he continued. "I can't help but feel that you

deceived me by omission. The past few weeks, you've had the opportunity to tell me and you didn't."

Trust was very important to Jared. Maybe it was everything in a relationship. She could see how betrayed he felt. She'd been afraid to trust him and now that might have damaged everything they had together.

What did you have? a small voice asked.

She had a connection with Jared that had been growing deeper and deeper, and now she didn't know if he wanted to be connected to her at all.

To save them both further embarrassment, she rose and picked up her purse. "I'd better go. I'll see you at work tomorrow."

He stood, too. "I'll be at the hospital in the morning, but I'll talk to my partners in the afternoon."

As of tomorrow afternoon, she might not have a job. She couldn't blame Jared for that. It was her own fault.

He walked her to the door, looking as much in turmoil as she felt.

"I'll see you tomorrow."

Tears lodged in her throat and she couldn't speak. She just nodded. When she reached her car, she told herself not to look back, but she did.

Why couldn't she learn that once something was lost, it couldn't be found again?

When Emily opened the door to the receptionist's office the next morning, Nancy stared at her as if she'd grown two heads and remarked, "I didn't think you'd come in this morning."

Emily had been dodging messages from the media on her answering machine. She'd also had to sneak out the back of her house this morning. Last night she'd parked on the street behind it to avoid a news van at the front curb.

"Did a reporter slip in here, too?"

"No. But you're on the news. Check MSNBC. They'll run through the cycle and you'll see it."

"Cycle?"

"Of breaking news. You were on last night. The footage was from someone's camera phone."

"But nobody knew who I was!"

"Someone must have written down your car license as you drove away."

So that's how they'd tracked her down. Not through Jared.

Emily went into the waiting room where a flat-screen TV hung on the wall to keep patients occupied while they were waiting. Now she switched the channel to MSNBC.

"This footage isn't the best," one of the anchors was saying as Emily saw a fuzzy image of herself kneeling beside Patti after the baby's birth. "A shopper downloaded this video to us from her cell phone," the anchor went on. "The woman who delivered the baby in the cereal aisle was Emily Diaz. Apparently there has been some controversy surrounding Ms. Diaz, who was once a midwife. A lawsuit was brought against her in Corpus Christi. Now, however, she works as an obstetrical nurse practitioner for Dr. Jared Madison at the Family Tree Health Center in Lubbock, Texas. More on this story as it unfolds. Now we have breaking news concerning the wildfires in Colorado."

Emily suddenly felt as if she'd entered an alternate universe. She was shaking all over. Her lawsuit was a matter of public record. It had been covered in the Corpus Christi papers.

"Emily? Are you okay?" Nancy asked, coming out from her cubicle.

"I'm fine," she murmured, not feeling fine at all. She turned away from the TV. "I'll be in my office if—"

"Your first two appointments canceled this morning," Nancy said in a rush as if she didn't want to deliver the news.

"Did they reschedule?" Emily hoped beyond hope the cancellations had nothing to do with the cable channel broadcast.

"Both Mrs. Janssen and Mrs. Davis said they'd only see Dr. Madison…or someone other than you."

With Jared's tight schedule, there was no way her appointments could be worked into his. She imagined the same was true for the other two obstetricians and their nurses. There was only one thing for her to do. The practice used nurses from a staffing agency when they got into a bind. There were two nurses at the agency who'd covered for vacations. Emily was going to find out if one of them was available.

Within the next fifteen minutes, she had done what she had to do. Her appointments could be covered. If any patients called in to reschedule, Nancy could tell them Emily was no longer working there.

Emily gathered her few possessions and put them into a box. Afterward, she sat at her computer, typed a letter, placed it in an envelope, which she laid in the center of Jared's desk blotter. She stared at it a few moments, then returned to her office and gathered her belongings. Soon she'd be home where she could pull the shades, turn off the phone and lock the doors.

Soon she'd be home where the reality that she might never see Jared Madison again might sink in.

Chapter Nine

Emily sat on the sofa, the evening paper folded on her lap, sadness washing over her in waves as she stared down at the article. Everyone in Sagebrush now knew what had happened to her in Corpus Christi. The reporter had made a point of explaining that neither the licensing board nor the jury had found any evidence of wrong doing against her, but would that make a difference? Could she find another job here in her field?

When Emily's doorbell rang, she was tempted to ignore it. Two news vans were still parked at the curb.

But then the doorbell rang again and was accompanied by a *knock, knock, knock.* "Emily, it's Jared. Open the door."

Jared. She thought maybe he'd just accept her resignation and her exit from his life. But if he was *here*—

She hurried from the sofa, rushed into the foyer and unlocked the door.

Jared stood there, his hair disheveled as if he'd run his hand through it a number of times. "I had two deliveries this afternoon. I got here as soon as I could. We have to talk."

"About my resignation?"

"Among other things. Can I come in?"

A member of a news crew started up the walk.

"Come in," she said, grabbing Jared's arm and tugging him inside as she slammed shut the door.

They stood together in the foyer, her fingers around his forearm, heat already prickling under her palm and up her hand. She released her hold.

He looked uncomfortable. "I talked to my partners about your resignation. Just for the record, I didn't agree with it."

"*You* didn't?"

"No, but they did," he said with an edge of disgust. "They're doubting your professional abilities. They don't like the cloud that's hanging over you, as you said. They're putting the reputation of the practice first and it's two against one. I'm sorry, Emily."

She had hoped…

What had she hoped? That they'd beg her to come back? That she was too valuable to lose?

Her gaze met Jared's. Her lower lip quivered and tears filled her eyes.

Jared suddenly hung his arm around her shoulders, then pulled her to his chest and just held her. "Everything will be all right."

She looked up at him. "Not if I can't find a job."

"Come on." He guided her to the living room. "Let's talk."

"About me keeping a secret from you? You'll never look at me the same way." She was so sad about that, so sorry if she'd hurt him. "After we got…involved, I knew I should tell you. But I was afraid to."

Jared tugged her down onto the sofa with him. "I should have been more understanding yesterday. Everyone has a past and a private life. Sometimes secrets are involved and sometimes they aren't. I reacted so strongly because... secrets hurt."

He looked away for a few moments, then returned his gaze to hers. "When I was a kid growing up, I thought I had an ordinary childhood. My mom worked part-time but was at home when I got home from school, baked cookies, always listened. My dad coached my Little League team. But when I was ten, I was in an automobile accident with my dad. He wasn't injured, but I had to have my spleen removed. He offered to donate blood for my surgery and found out his blood type and mine weren't compatible. Wyatt wasn't my father."

Emily could hardly imagine that shock for a ten-year-old...that type of crisis. Forgetting her own problems, she covered his hand with hers and asked softly, "What happened?"

"It turns out, my mom was engaged to Wyatt when an old boyfriend returned to Lubbock for a business conference. They had dinner. One thing led to another.... When she became pregnant, she wanted the baby to be Wyatt's. But when I was born, she asked about my blood type and knew I wasn't. She'd kept the secret from both of us all those years. From then on their marriage was damaged. Two years later, they divorced."

He had summed up the emotional trauma, but those years must have been chaotic. "Did you search for your biological father?"

Jared leaned back against the sofa and replied dispassionately, "Years later. Reunions don't always work. I was twenty by then, and at that point, my father had a family and didn't need another son. We didn't connect. He wasn't interested."

On top of everything that had happened, Jared had been rejected by his biological father! "And your stepdad?"

"After he found out, our relationship changed. I saw him once a month, but nothing was the same. He looked at me differently, and I knew he was thinking I *wasn't* his son. After a year or so, he moved to Arizona, and I only visited once a year. When I was in med school, he had a heart attack. I went to see him and our relationship got stronger. But he died a few years ago."

"I'm so sorry."

Jared must have questioned everything about who he was and where he belonged.

"I think what happened when I was small pushed me to choose medicine and to focus too much on my career. That's why my marriage didn't work. My career took up too much of my time. If Valerie hadn't felt so overburdened…"

His voice lowered as if the telling of this was difficult. "The girls were a year old when Valerie asked me to take care of them for a few weeks so she could take the trip of her dreams to South America. I agreed. She died while she was there."

"Oh, Jared."

"She didn't tell me she had pancreatic cancer. She didn't tell me she only had a few months to live. She made sure she left when she knew the end was near. I'm a doctor, Emily. How blind could I have been? More important, why couldn't she have trusted me to take care of her at the end? I could have gotten her the best medical care."

"She wanted you to be with your daughters. She wanted their lives to be as normal as possible."

"She didn't trust me to help her…and she died alone."

Because of what Jared had revealed, she understood him so much better.

Side-by-side with him on the sofa, she could feel his strength. But now she also knew his vulnerability. "How are you able to trust?"

"I don't trust many people. They have to earn it."

And she hadn't. She'd kept important information from him. She asked, "Why did you come over?"

Her heart was beating so fast she could hardly breathe. Maybe he'd come to end everything they'd had together once and for all.

"I went back to the articles in the Corpus Christi papers, the editorials, the letters to the editor. Everybody had an opinion. But I know the statistics on stillborn births. The autopsy showed nothing. The mother had presented no alerting symptoms. Everything was fine until it wasn't. Being a midwife or a doctor wouldn't have changed that."

"You're so sure?"

"I'm sure...because I *know* you. You trust your intuition. At the first sign of anything amiss, you would have called for help."

She saw the respect in his eyes, the certainty that he trusted her as a professional. But did she see something else, too? Something that went beyond their professional relationship?

His voice was husky when he said, "I hate the idea of you leaving the practice. Number one—because you're damn good at your job. But number two—I'm going to miss seeing you there every day."

A lump formed in her throat. She pushed words past it. "I'm going to miss you, too."

As she gazed into Jared's eyes, she felt everything she'd experienced from the first day she'd met him. Current that had made her heart race and her hands tremble vibrated now between them. But along with it was so much more—admiration for Jared as a dad, respect for him as a doctor. And suddenly she knew she loved him whether she should or shouldn't, whether it was risky or not, whether the time was right or the time was wrong. She ached for him to touch her, hold her, love her.

When Jared opened his arms to her, she didn't hesitate to nestle against his chest, to let his strength flow into her. He lifted her chin and his lips came down on hers in a kiss that was hungry and aching. Neither of them knew what would happen next or where their lives would lead them. She wanted to experience everything she could with him right now. She kissed him back as if tomorrow would never come, as if the universe could stop, stay at this point forever, and she'd be perfectly happy. Desire they'd both been keeping at bay ran rampant. His firm exploration of her mouth, his hands in her hair, his groan of satisfaction when she returned every enthusiastic stroke of his tongue told him she had no doubts about what they were doing, no doubts about anything more they might want to do.

Jared broke the kiss to gaze at her, his eyes filled with hungry desire. "I want you, Emily. If we keep this up, we're going to be naked on the sofa again. Is that what you want?"

"I think naked sounds good," she teased, letting him know she wanted this. "But we'd have more privacy if we went to my room."

Jared smiled, tugged her to her feet then swept her up into his arms. "Which way?"

She told herself this wasn't a dream. She told herself they still had issues to settle. She told herself to forget about everything but now.

Jared carried her up the steps to her bedroom. The

yellow-and-white plaid curtains, the white chenille spread gave a pristine look to the room. But Emily's crafting yarns and needles spread on a card table, her collection of perfume bottles on the dresser, the large print of a little girl and boy sitting at the beach on the edge of the shore, personalized the space as Emily's.

Jared held her in his arms looking around the room. Then his gaze came back to her. "I like who you are."

She laid her hand on the side of his cheek, ran her thumb over his jaw. "I like who *you* are."

Her words broke any thread still binding his restraint. His lips came down on hers possessively and she welcomed them; she welcomed him. Still kissing her, he set her down next to the bed.

They kissed as he undressed her, long, wet, erotic kisses that made her head spin. Finally he broke away and lifted her blouse over her head. His fingers whispered over her skin as they found the clasp of her bra. When he bent his head and kissed her breasts, her knees almost buckled. His hot lips on her skin made her whole body tingle, and when his tongue touched her nipple, she thought she'd come apart.

But Jared knew how to keep the anticipation building. He kissed down her stomach to her navel, and then he removed her slacks. He would have gone further, but she stayed his hands. "My turn to do half of you."

He laughed, dropped his hands to his sides and let her pleasure him. She unbuttoned his shirt and kissed his chest. He sucked in a breath as her lips trailed lower to his waist.

"Maybe we should move on to something else," he said huskily.

"No problem," she teased as she unfastened his belt. By doing that, it was as if she unlocked all of his hunger and everything he'd been holding back.

A few minutes later, he'd completely undressed her, rid himself of the rest of his clothes and lay beside her in the bed where she'd spent so many nights alone.

She supposed what surprised her most was that Jared *cared* about her pleasure. He seemed to revel in the sighs that came from her mouth, the small moans she couldn't keep in, the trembling that invaded her whole body the longer he kissed and touched and caressed.

When he stretched out on top of her, he didn't enter her. Rather he rocked against her slowly, erotically, increasing her anticipation and her need.

"Jared!" She dug her fingers into his shoulders.

"What?" he asked, and she thought she heard amusement in his question.

"I want…I want…"

"Tell me," he requested, still sliding his body against hers, still making her crazy.

"I want *you* inside me."

"That's what I want, too." Then he entered her with the same lazy slowness that he'd used to bring her to complete arousal.

She wrapped her legs around him to take him deeper. When he groaned, she knew she was doing something right. This wasn't the mechanical lovemaking she'd experienced with her husband. This was exciting and exhilarating and even scary in its intensity.

He kissed her neck, took her earlobe between his lips and that's when it happened. Without warning, her whole body tightened. She felt suspended between the present and the future. Then in an erotic rush, she was overcome by a deluge of sensation that sent fire to her nerve endings, made her heart race as if she'd run a marathon and left her shaking with pleasure, dancing from her head to her toes.

She called Jared's name and held on, never wanting the glorious rush of feeling to end. He thrust into her again and again. Her muscles contracted around him and embraced him as if he belonged in her life.

Jared's shudder and deep groan signaled his release. He collapsed on top of her, his fingers lacing in her hair.

"That was incredible," he rasped into her neck.

All she could do was rub her cheek against his in agreement, reveling in the sensation of his beard stubble, loving everything about what had happened between them.

They were still holding each other, still floating in the aftermath of excellent lovemaking, when Emily heard the crunch of a car on gravel outside on the driveway to the detached garage.

Jared felt her stiffen. "What's wrong?"

"Francesca's home. It will only take her a few minutes to lock up the garage and come into the house."

"Do you want to pretend this didn't happen?" Jared asked, withdrawing from her, rolling onto his side.

She reached out and touched his shoulder. "No. But I'd like to be dressed when she comes in."

He took Emily's hand and kissed her palm. That kiss started her nerve endings tingling all over again.

"I'm a fast dresser," he assured her.

Emily scrambled from the bed, hurriedly picked up her underwear, bra, slacks and blouse and dashed into the bathroom next door. When she returned to the bedroom to slip on her shoes, Jared was dressed and waiting for her.

They heard the front door open and then close. "Emily?" Francesca called.

"Up here," Emily called back, then added, "Jared's with me."

There was silence on the first floor as she and Jared

went down the steps and found Francesca standing in the foyer waiting for them.

"Hello, Jared," her friend said, unable to suppress a small smile.

"Francesca," he acknowledged, his complexion a bit ruddier than usual.

"There are two news vans outside with anchors who want interviews with you—*both* of you."

The phone rang again and after the third ring, the answering machine in the living room clicked on. "Miss Diaz, this is Cindy Sanchez, from the *Amarillo Herald*. We'd like to do a human interest piece on you. Please give me a call." The reporter left her number.

Francesca shook her head. "Where's your car? Still over on Monterey?"

Emily nodded. "I snuck in the back way earlier."

Jared said to Francesca, "Will you excuse us for a minute?"

"Sure. I need to grab something to eat. I'll be in the kitchen."

As soon as Francesca disappeared, Jared said, "Why don't you come home with me? I know the girls would like to see you. You can stay the night and get away from all this."

"Won't you have reporters at your place?"

"No. I already gave an interview. They're not going to bother with me. We can go out the back and take your car. I'll pick up mine tomorrow."

She liked the idea of going home with him, of seeing Courtney and Amy again. "If I go home with you—"

"You're welcome to sleep in my bedroom with me," he finished with a grin.

She'd like nothing better. But she didn't know what

sleeping with Jared meant. Her turmoil must have been obvious.

"Or you can sleep in the guest room. No strings, Emily. If you just want a place to hide out for a while, I can give you that. Francesca can tell the news vans you're not here and they'll leave."

It did sound like a temporary solution. But she didn't want Francesca to feel as if she were deserting her and leaving her with the results of her own situation.

However, Francesca thought it was a great idea. She had no qualms about telling the reporters that Emily had left. She assured Emily, "In a few days, something else will catch their interest and they'll all forget about you."

Emily could only hope that was true.

A short time later, as Jared drove Emily's car to his house, she glanced at him because he seemed lost in thought. Was he regretting what had happened between them? Was he regretting getting involved? She wanted to ask him, but did she really want to know the answer?

There were no reporters at Jared's. Chloie's car sat in his driveway. Jared came around to her side of the car to open the door for her. He offered her his hand to help her out. His long, warm fingers wrapped around hers and she explicitly remembered every stroke, every caress, every sensation in her bedroom.

Her cheeks must have taken on some color because he gave her a crooked half smile and said, "We're good together."

What was there to say to that?

She followed him up the step to the porch and suddenly he stopped before opening the door. "I want to ask you something before we go inside."

"What?" Was he going to ask her again to share his bed?

She was so tempted to say yes, but she knew she shouldn't for a multitude of reasons.

"I want you to think about accepting a different job than the one you've been doing."

She waited.

"Chloie's work is backing up, but she doesn't want to leave me stranded. My mother's coming home soon. Obviously she won't be able to help with the girls until she gets back on her feet. Will you stay with me to care for the twins and give my mother a helping hand? I'll pay you a salary commensurate with what you were getting at the office."

"Oh, Jared, you don't have to do that."

"I could call a nanny service. I could call a nursing aide service. But I know the girls like you, and I think my mother does, too. What do you say?"

She realized how much she wanted him to ask her to stay for personal reasons rather than practical ones. She'd already decided she wouldn't share his bed with him... because of his daughters...because they both needed some breathing room. But they could really get to know each other if she stayed. On the other hand, living with Jared would be risking her heart.

No risk, no reward, she reminded herself. "I'll have to speak to Francesca about it. I don't want her to feel I'm deserting her. If she's okay with the idea, yes, I'll take care of the girls and your mom for as long as you need me."

With a slow smile turning up the corners of his lips, he bent to her and kissed her.

No risk, no reward, she reminded herself again.

But as his kiss excited and aroused her, she knew if she risked and lost this time, she might never recover.

Chapter Ten

Amy tugged on Emily's hand. "Isn't Daddy coming?"

Would Jared manage to get away for the girls' preschool open house? He'd e-mailed their teacher that Emily would be standing in for him if he was delayed.

They'd gone to separate rooms last night. But that's what she'd told him she wanted, wasn't it? Wouldn't the girls be confused if they saw her with their dad in his bedroom? His daughters had to be the priority.

Other children in the preschool class showed their parents their projects hanging on the corkboard strips or sitting on the table in the back of the room.

"Your dad must have gotten tied up. I know he'd be here if he could be."

Courtney nodded her head solemnly. "He's helping a baby come out of a mommy's tummy."

That about summed it up, Emily thought, knowing

Jared would regret missing this. But she was glad she could be here for the girls. As they grew older, they'd understand better about their dad's erratic hours…and his dedication.

After a snack of carrots, grapes and apples, Emily said good-bye to their teacher and was walking Amy and Courtney to the car when Jared zoomed into the parking lot and parked his sedan next to her car. Many of the parents had already left. She was one of the last, lingering in case he would arrive.

"Daddy!" Courtney and Amy yelled as Jared climbed out of his car, and they scrambled toward him and hugged him.

"Come on!" Courtney tugged on his arm. "You can see our pictures."

When Jared crossed to Emily, the girls hanging on either side of him, the look he gave her made all of her nerve endings stand up and take notice.

His hair blew in the wind as his gaze slid over her russet pantsuit. "Am I too late?"

"Not if you hurry. Why don't you take them inside and I'll go back to the house and get lunch ready? Can you stay for lunch?"

"I have a break before afternoon hours. Are you sure you don't want to come in with us?"

She didn't want the girls' teacher to assume something that wasn't a reality. She also didn't want Jared to feel awkward with her by his side, and he might. So she said, "I've already seen it all."

She gave the girls quick hugs. "I'll meet you back at your house."

They returned her embrace, and all over again she was filled with the desire to be their "real" mom.

A half hour later, Jared and the twins were back at

home. The girls ran into their room to play. Jared's expression was unreadable as he unbuttoned his jacket and hung it around a kitchen chair.

"How did it go?" she asked.

"Mrs. Lannigan couldn't spend much time with me. She had a meeting."

"I wrote down everything she told me. Would you like to see my notes?" Emily would have passed by Jared to fetch her purse on the counter, but he caught her arm.

"Just tell me." His voice was husky and low, sending a tremble up her spine.

Emily fought to remember everything she'd written down, even though his presence was wrapping her thoughts in a gauzy haze. "I think Mrs. Lannigan connects with Amy and Courtney. She's warm and sweet and tries to really listen to them. She says they're playing with the other children but their main bond is with each other. Courtney seems to depend on that more than Amy."

Jared was listening closely and she went on. "Amy loves the crafts projects and Courtney is fascinated by numbers. Mrs. Lannigan feels they take direction well and are fast learners. I think that's a great report, really. What did she tell you?"

"That they're a joy to have in the classroom. I didn't have time to look at all their projects," he said with a frown. He was still holding her arm. Now he moved his hand to her shoulder. "Were you upset when I wasn't there on time?"

Her answer came out spontaneously. "No, I wasn't upset. I knew you had a delivery this morning and there's never any way of knowing how long that will take."

"It didn't bother you that you had to have the meeting with Mrs. Lannigan?"

"No," she said again. "That's why I took notes. I was standing in for you and didn't want to miss anything she told me."

Jared's expression was pensive as he assessed her answer, she supposed looking for the truth. She had nothing to hide. He knew all of her secrets now.

"Were the twins upset?" he asked.

"I'm sure they were disappointed. Amy asked if you were coming, but I think they understood. I told them you got tied up at the hospital."

"Do you think they'll ever really understand? I might miss more than a preschool open house. There might be sports events, recitals."

"I think you're getting ahead of yourself. You might be able to attend as many as you miss."

"While you're here, caring for them, I don't want you to feel I'm taking advantage of you. Valerie never understood the demands of what I do."

Ever since Jared had told her about his ex-wife, she'd suspected he'd bottled up many feelings that had caused him to pull back from other women and remove himself from the dating process. But did he want to talk about it now? Should she take the chance? "What did she expect?"

He dropped his hand from her shoulder. "She expected me to call another doctor to take over for me. I couldn't just opt out any time I wanted. She didn't understand the planning involved in a practice, the sense of responsibility to a patient."

Emily didn't know whether to say what she was thinking or not, but she did. "I understand about delivering babies, Jared. I understand it very well. There's more to caring for a pregnant mom than just running into the delivery room, delivering the baby and running out again."

"Valerie got upset when I'd miss a dinner with friends, a play she'd bought tickets for, a concert that happened to be on one of my on-call weekends."

"Did she understand what a doctor's life was like when she married you?"

"I think at the time all she was concerned about was the security of our life, that I was making an income that would provide a house and a cushion so that we could have kids and pay for their college education. She was looking at the big picture, not what the details of my schedule would do to her plans. Sometimes I think she didn't tell me about her illness out of resentment for all the times I disappointed her."

Emily's voice grew very soft. "And maybe she didn't tell you because she wanted to spare you."

He cupped her cheek. "Somehow you always make me feel better. I can't stay away from you, but I don't want to coax you into an affair that might not be the relationship you want."

"Oh, Jared. Don't you think I'm old enough to make up my own mind?"

"Sometimes our minds give way to our needs. I've never met anyone like you, Emily." He tipped her head up and his lips came down hard on hers.

Need was there—the need to possess, the need to have drives fulfilled, the need for pleasure. She wasn't sure what other needs she could taste, but she did know her need was as great as his.

His hands passed down her back and cupped her buttocks. She pressed against him, feeling his arousal, wanting to satisfy hers.

The telephone rang.

Jared broke the kiss and swore, pressing his forehead against hers, kissing the side of her neck. "I'll check caller ID," he said, reluctantly breaking away.

When he picked up the cordless phone, he said to Emily, "It's the rehab center. I have to take this."

Emily listened as he said, "Mom, are you sure you're all right?"

There must have been an explanation for her call because it took a few moments.

His brow furrowed. "They're certain you're ready to come home?"

A shorter pause.

"All right. I'll clear my schedule from eleven until one the day after tomorrow and bring you home. As we discussed last night, Emily will be here to help you. You'd like to speak to her? She's right here. Hold on." He handed the phone over to Emily, then leaned against the counter, waiting.

Emily took the phone. "Hello, Mrs. Madison."

"Emily, dear, it's Gloria. I just want to make sure you want to do this. Taking care of Amy and Courtney might be enough for you to handle."

"Do you feel comfortable being here with me, and depending on me for a while?" Emily asked, knowing that his mom's confidence in her was important.

"This could be a few weeks," Gloria reminded her. "Maybe longer."

"I'm sure each day you'll grow stronger. Jared said we can arrange your physical therapy appointments for the days the girls have preschool. And if we need another time in the week, Chloie will watch them. We've got all the bases covered. You just have to come home and get better."

There was a short silence, then Gloria's voice sounded full of emotion. "You know what? I think I'm going to like having you around. If you're sure this isn't too much to take on."

"It's not too much."

"Jared explained about that article in the paper and what happened. You must be so disappointed to have lost your job. But this is only temporary, you know. You have to go back to doing what you do best."

"I need a little time to make some decisions."

"I have a favor to ask you. I've already spoken to Jared about it. My occupational therapist would like you to come in so she can speak with you about how I'll manage when I'm home. Will you come?"

"Of course I'll come. When?"

"Tomorrow morning while the twins are in preschool. Around ten?"

"Ten will be fine. Now you take care of yourself and I'll see you tomorrow."

After she handed the phone back to Jared, he conversed with his mother a few more minutes, then hung up. "I think my mother has already decided that she likes you. That's a good thing. She'll be more cooperative."

Jared always sounded a little removed when he talked about his mother. She wished he could forgive his mom for the secret she'd kept.

"I like your mom, and we'll get along."

"Once my mother's here, we'll have few opportunities for privacy. After the twins are asleep tonight, maybe we should take advantage of it." He brought Emily back into his arms and kissed her again. Jared indeed wanted privacy for them. Would intimacy lead him to love? Or would it lead him to satisfy his physical needs and deny his emotional ones?

She'd only know with time. She'd only know by risking her heart.

* * *

Jared drove home from the hospital the following night, feeling as if his whole life was changing. Yet nothing had changed...not really.

You had sex again, a voice inside his head reminded him.

Yes, he had. Very good sex. And he wanted to have it again and again. He rationalized that he could compartmentalize. He could enjoy going to bed with Emily yet not get tangled up in a committed relationship. At least that's what he was telling himself whenever he was near her... whenever he kissed her.

Being around Emily dredged up unwelcome memories. Memories of a time before his mother and Wyatt divorced... when they'd seemed to be a happy family. Years had passed since he'd willingly examined what had happened in his childhood. His mother had destroyed their family and his sense of identity. He'd thought Wyatt was his father, like any other kid's dad. He'd thought his mother had loved Wyatt and that's why they'd gotten married and had him. Had she loved Wyatt? Or had she really loved the man she'd had an affair with? His mother had known the truth from his birth, but she had deceived him, as well as Wyatt, to hold on to a life that was a lie.

Jared knew his mother had been trying to make up for the rift between them by taking care of his daughters, by being the best grandmother she knew how to be. Courtney and Amy loved her. Yet he couldn't get past the pain of losing a father and, in a sense, of losing a mother, too.

And then there was Emily. What about her omission on her résumé?

Had she lied? Or had she merely not revealed all? Was that the same as a lie?

He didn't know anymore. Emily seemed to understand him. She didn't judge him. Because she accepted him the way he was?

He didn't know why he felt such turmoil. Again he told himself nothing had changed.

Yet Emily was taking care of his daughters. The same tempting person he wanted to keep at arm's length was living in his house.

He opened the garage with the remote, pulled in and sat in the car, thinking about his marriage and divorce. Whereas Valerie had hated his erratic hours, Emily seemed to take them in stride. He knew without a doubt that if he and Valerie had planned to go to the preschool open house and he'd had to deliver a baby instead, she would have been disappointed and hurt and accusing. She would have insisted his career always came before his family.

Emily seemed to understand his dedication. And she understood the miracle of birth.

Still, once his mother was back on her feet, he wouldn't need Emily, at least not to take care of his daughters. He didn't want to need her any other way, either. Relationships of any kind ultimately caused heartache. He was invested in his daughters' lives, and that was enough. As they grew up, they'd have both rough and smooth roads to travel. He was ready for that. He was committed to them. He didn't need any more commitments or want them.

He felt calmed by the thought that his direction was mapped out with certainty once more. He opened the sedan's door, climbed out and headed for the two steps leading into the house.

When he opened the kitchen door, he listened and all

seemed to be quiet. It was almost 11:00 p.m. Had Emily waited up for him or gone to bed?

However, as he crossed the kitchen, he heard a sound and stopped. It was a sound that always seemed to tear his heart apart. Courtney was crying.

Hurrying through the dining area and the great room, he went down the hall to the girls' room. He stopped in the doorway.

Emily sat beside Courtney in her bed, her arms around the little girl. She was stroking Courtney's hair and murmuring to her.

When Amy saw him, she sidled down to the bottom of her bed. "Hi, Daddy." She held her arms up to him.

He didn't hesitate to scoop her up and hold her tight, just as Emily was holding Courtney. Both of his girls needed him, but Emily was taking care of one of them, and he was grateful for that.

Only a Snow White night-light in the wall socket cast a glow into the room. He and Emily sat there, holding the girls, glancing at each other now and then, until Courtney's cries subsided. Emily wiped away his daughter's tears and settled her in the bed, tucking the covers around her.

Afterward, she kissed his little girl's forehead and crossed to Amy to give her a squeeze, too. "See you in the morning. Blueberry pancakes?"

Amy nodded and Emily left the room.

Jared tucked in Amy, brushed her hair over her forehead and then kissed her cheek. "Good night, honey."

"Are you going to have blueberry pancakes, too?" she asked sleepily.

"I just might do that."

Moments later, after he'd made sure Courtney was sleeping once more, he found Emily in the kitchen unloading the dishwasher. He walked over to her and put his hand on her shoulder. "Thank you."

As she looked up at him, her brown eyes still filled with compassion for Courtney, she replied, "No thanks are necessary."

The hood light over the stove illuminated the kitchen with a soft yellow glow. With his being this close to Emily, witnessing her empathy for his daughter, the desire to hold her seemed overwhelming. Yet too many questions plagued him. What would an affair accomplish? His girls were quickly becoming attached to Emily in a way they were never attached to anyone else. Did he really want that? Did he want her to mother his children?

Even if he did, what happened when she left? What happened when she decided his hours were too long, or the affection he gave her wasn't enough, or the daughters who weren't hers were taking up too much of her time? He didn't have any answers. All he had were doubts.

Stepping away from Emily and the temptation she represented, the hopes she represented, he realized hope was as risky as happiness. He couldn't get a grasp on it.

"You don't have to do that now," he said roughly, gesturing to the clean dishes.

If she had been expecting another kiss, she didn't show it. Her smile seemed a little forced. "You're right. I'll have the girls help me in the morning. They like to feel useful."

She seemed to think about his daughters as if she were their mother. But she wasn't.

After she pushed in the rack on the dishwasher and closed it, he switched off the hood light over the stove. They walked down the hall to their bedrooms.

At his door he said, "I'll see you in the morning."

"Morning," she agreed, and then went into her room.

He wanted to say *Wait, come into mine.* He wanted to pull her into his bed and make love to her again.

But if he did, she'd know he needed her. She'd know he couldn't stay away from her. And that would be leading her on.

Emily didn't deserve that. He couldn't give her what she did deserve—promises that stretched beyond one night.

Chapter Eleven

Emily was waiting in the living room when Jared brought his mother home. Gloria was using a walker. The occupational therapist had assured Emily that Gloria should use it until she felt comfortable with a cane.

"You're doing terrific," Emily said warmly as Gloria maneuvered into the great room.

When Emily glanced at Jared, she couldn't read his expression. He'd been quiet today. Maybe he was concerned about how his mother would get around.

Amy and Courtney scurried toward Gloria, each carrying a rose that Emily had bought at the florist's.

"Oh, how pretty." Gloria gave the twins the biggest hugs she could.

"I'll put them in your room," Emily offered. "Would you like to go there now, or settle on the sofa?"

"Probably your room would be best," Jared remarked.

"I bought one of those lift chairs to make it easier for you to get up and down. You've had a long morning."

His mom did look a little tired.

"Can Grandma play a game with us?" Amy asked her dad.

He stooped down, took Amy in one arm and Courtney in the other. "Did you have your lunch?"

They both nodded.

"Then why don't I take you two to the park while Grandma settles in and rests a bit? There will be plenty of time to play games later. I promise."

Emily stood by Gloria's side and felt the older woman lean more on her walker. She touched her elbow. "Are you all right?"

"Just a little wobbly sometimes. Maybe I'd better head for my room."

They all walked her to her bedroom. When she reached it, she spotted the oversized recliner that had replaced the bedroom chair. It sat near the window so she could look out at the yard.

"Let me show you how it works," Jared told her, lifting the control. As he demonstrated, he explained, "It has heat and a massager."

"Oh, Jared. That's so kind. Thank you." She put her arms around her son.

He hugged her back, but not for very long. Stepping away, he almost looked embarrassed. "It's the least I can do for all you've done for the girls."

"Taking care of them has been a joy, and it will be again. Now I think I'll try out my new chair." Gloria sank down onto it, pressed the button until the back reclined a bit and the footrest came up. "I think I could get too used to this," she said with a small laugh.

"Did you have lunch?" Emily asked her.

"No, I didn't."

"I made the girls sandwiches and I have extras. I'll fix you a plate. Jared, how about you?"

"I'm fine."

Sometimes Emily felt Jared was an island and the sea around him was just too deep to cross.

"Go get your shoes," Jared told his daughters.

They ran for their bedroom.

He and his mother and Emily were alone, and the atmosphere was awkward.

Finally, Gloria said, "I don't want you two treating me as an invalid. I have to do things on my own. If I can't do them, I'll ask for help. But otherwise, give me a chance. That's what rehab was all about. Agreed?"

Emily gave a nod. "Agreed."

"Of course," Jared assured her, then moved toward the door. "I'm going to get the girls and go." He focused on his mother. "Take this time to rest and whenever the girls tire you out, I want you to let us know."

This time Gloria wasn't so fast to respond. "They'll have to tire me out a great deal for me to let you know."

Jared shook his head and left the room.

A few seconds later, Amy and Courtney peeked in and waved good-bye. Then the women heard the front door close.

"I'll get you lunch."

"I have a feeling you're going to spoil me."

Emily crouched down beside Gloria's chair. "I think someone should. You've done a wonderful job taking care of Amy and Courtney. And you raised Jared into a fine man."

"You know, don't you?" Gloria asked.

Emily wasn't going to play dumb. "I know some things."

"You know I had a fling while I was engaged to Wyatt."

Emily nodded.

"In that case, you also know why Wyatt divorced me. Jared believes his life was never the same after that…and it wasn't."

"Yes, I know that, too. I'm sorry for all you went through…for all Jared went through. It must have been a traumatic time for all of you."

"It was. I'd kept the secret far too long. Jared had every right to feel betrayed and angry and resentful, just as Wyatt did. Jared lost the only father he'd ever known."

"But he still saw him."

"Yes, but their relationship changed."

"It shouldn't have. He was his father in the real sense."

"I think they both came to realize that before Wyatt died. But neither of them ever forgave me and I don't blame them."

Emily shook her head. "Life's too short to keep blaming someone for what they did wrong. I lost both of my parents. Jared doesn't realize how lucky he is to still have you."

"And how about you, Emily? Does Jared realize how lucky he is to have you?"

She felt her cheeks flush and rose to her feet. The motion gave her a few moments to think because she wasn't sure what to say.

"Don't feel you have to be guarded with me, dear. I know what Jared's like. I know he protects himself. Did he tell you about Valerie?"

"Yes, he did. So I understand why he's reluctant to get involved with anyone."

"She was mistaken to run away like that. It hurt him, and I'm afraid he thinks knowing she left him like that will hurt Amy and Courtney someday. He worries about the right time to tell them."

"Maybe the right time is when they start asking. But even then, he needs to give only as much as they can understand."

"Exactly." Gloria smiled. "You *are* good for him."

"You don't know that."

"I know that he never trusted the girls with anyone but me and Chloie."

"I'll only be here until you're back on your feet. This is only temporary. I hope to work in my field again, if anyone will hire me."

"You have doubts because of that newspaper story?"

"What happened to me in Corpus Christi was on the news, too."

"Listen, Emily. You delivered a baby in a grocery store. You did a good job of it. That just proves that you were a good midwife."

"No, it proved Patti had an easy birth."

"Have you seen her since that day?"

"Too much press. I didn't want to subject her to that. I came here to stay with Jared because of the reporters outside my house. But then he asked me to stay and care for the girls while you recuperated. But after you've recovered, I'll have to find work again."

"You'll find a job. But in your heart, you have to know what you really want to do with your career…with Jared. If you have feelings for him, you might have to poke a few holes in those walls of his."

Poke a few holes. Emily had no idea how to do that. But she did know his mother had just given her the courage to try.

Emily knew it was pretty obvious as she sat on the sofa watching TV that she was waiting for Jared. He'd been called to the hospital in the middle of dinner.

When the call had come in, he'd glanced at Emily and asked, "Are you going to be okay here with Mom and the girls?"

"Your mom is hardly any work at all, and I love putting the girls to bed."

"I can read to them, too," Gloria had interjected. "Just because I have to walk slowly doesn't mean I'm not capable."

Jared had raised his brows and then told his service he'd be at the hospital in ten minutes.

It was midnight now. Emily knew Jared would expect she'd be in bed, but she had a few questions for him she didn't feel could wait.

When she heard his key in the door, she went perfectly still.

He apparently spotted the light still shining in the great room. "I thought you'd be in bed."

"I'm not sleepy. How about you? How was the delivery?"

He came over to the sofa and lowered himself beside her. With elbows propped on his knees, he rubbed his face with both hands and then glanced over at her. "It was a long, tough labor for the mom. The epidural didn't seem to help as much as it should have. I began to wonder if something was wrong even though none of the monitors showed anything. Do you know what I mean? It was just a gut feeling."

"I know what you mean."

She could feel the heat of Jared's body. They were sitting that close. He looked as if he might want to reach over and touch her, but he didn't.

"What happened?"

"The fetal heart rate changed. I did a cesarean. The cord was wrapped around the baby's neck."

Emily's breath caught.

"The baby's okay. We got him in time. The Apgar score was good." Jared sat up straighter, rolled his shoulders and his neck a couple of different ways.

You've got to poke holes in those walls.

Following her instincts, Emily said, "Take off your shirt and let me give you a massage."

He glanced at her. "I don't think that's a good idea."

"It's going to take you at least an hour to unwind, an hour that you could be sleeping. Just let me loosen up your muscles a bit."

He thought about her suggestion but not for very long. "Are you a pro at massages?"

"Actually, massage *was* part of my training. It helps women relax when they're in labor."

At that, he smiled and unbuttoned his shirt. As soon as he did, as soon as he pulled it from his trousers, rolled it into a ball and tossed it to the end of the sofa, Emily knew she was way in over her head. This wasn't going to poke holes in *his* walls. It was going to demolish *hers*. If she touched him again, she'd have no protection for her heart.

Did she want protection? Did she need protection? Or was she ready to take a risk to find happiness again?

"Why don't I sit over there?" He stood and went to the hassock, sitting with his tanned back facing her.

She took a deep breath, crossed to him and started with his neck, reaching around to his jaw. She felt his beard stubble as she smoothed her thumbs over tense muscles, using her fingers at pressure points, easing away knots, giving comfort and in measure, her love. She did love Jared.

He groaned when she moved to his shoulders, kneading them.

"No tension there," she commented dryly.

"That's where it all goes," he mumbled. "Did anyone ever tell you you have magic hands?"

"No."

"Well, I'm telling you. In fact…" He stopped. "Never mind."

She wished he would say what he was thinking. She wished he could trust her with his feelings…and his heart.

After kneading his shoulders and upper arm muscles, she began circling his shoulder blades, trying to keep the ministrations impersonal, almost professional. That was so impossible. This was Jared and she loved touching him.

Suddenly he turned around and caught her hands.

"What's wrong? Did I hurt you?"

"You're driving me crazy."

"Jared, I didn't mean to—"

She never finished her thought as he stood, pulled her arms around his waist and captured her lips with his. He was hungry for her as she was hungry for him. It seemed as if they'd been apart forever. His tongue slid from one corner of her mouth to the other and stroked her. She responded, kissing him back, with the depth of her growing feelings for him.

He broke the kiss but still held her tight and grumbled into her neck, "I'd take you right here but we know how foolish *that* would be." Then he scooped her up into his arms. "If we're quiet about this, no one has to know."

She knew what he meant. His mother, in the room next to his, could hear any sound.

As he carried her, she wondered what had happened to the questions she had wanted to ask him.

Maybe after they made love he'd answer her questions. Maybe after they made love she could tell him she loved him.

In Jared's bedroom, they silently skimmed off their

clothes. They had no words, no pillow talk, no expression of feelings. There was only a need that was stronger and bigger and wider and higher than they were.

Jared's large hands possessed all of her. He knew the fullness of her breasts, the roundness of her bottom, the length of her thighs, the narrowness of her feet. He touched her everywhere. The silence between them seemed to magnify every sensation, every push of their limbs on the sheet, every sigh that went no farther than her mouth to his.

They had made love before, kissed before, touched before. Tonight there was an urgency about it that made Emily wonder even more what Jared was thinking and feeling. Was he telling himself this was only sex? Was he reminding himself they were merely having an affair? Was he thinking this was the last time it would happen? Was he wondering where and when they could do it again?

After he brought them both to a sublime arousal, he pulled her astride him.

Their gazes met. Neither looked away. White moonlight invaded the room, illuminating their intertwined bodies.

As she slid onto him, Jared whispered her name. It was the only sound in the room, so hushed she didn't know if she'd really heard it. She rocked with him, contracted around him, tried to imagine his walls falling down. They inched closer and closer to the peak of pleasure.

She reached it first. The orgasm suspended her, shook her, invaded her...until heat was all that was left of an ecstatically erotic fire that had shot through her limbs.

Jared's body shuddered several times and she knew he'd found the same release. Had he felt the deep part of heat? Did it still claim him?

So many questions.

Yet they were silent as she slipped off him to lie beside him. He held her tightly in his arms, kissing her on the mouth, and then the temple. A few minutes later, from Jared's deep breathing, Emily realized he was asleep. She also realized she couldn't stay. If she let herself fall asleep beside him, she'd be here until morning. She couldn't take that chance.

Giving herself only a few more minutes of lying next to the man she loved, she slipped out of his arms and off the bed, collected her clothes, opened his door to make sure the hall was clear and then scurried to her bedroom.

Her questions would have to wait.

And Jared's walls?

Tomorrow she'd test them, to see if they'd weakened. If not?

She'd just have to try again.

Emily sat in the waiting room of the hospital's outpatient physical therapy center the following week, hoping no one recognized her. Francesca had told her no more reporters were calling the house. She was old news, thank goodness. With the girls at preschool, she'd brought Gloria to her appointment. But Emily couldn't keep her mind on the midwifery articles in her lap. She couldn't stop thinking about Jared.

As if she'd conjured him up, he strode into the reception area and made a beeline toward her.

She was suddenly worried. Had Mrs. Lannigan called him? "The girls are okay, aren't they? When I dropped them off at preschool they seemed fine."

"They're good as far as I know. This isn't an emergency visit," he replied with a smile. "I wanted to see how Mom was doing with her session."

This was supposed to be Jared's day off. But he usually checked on patients in the hospital even on his day off. She hoped he could snatch a few free hours.

Lowering himself into the chair beside her, he asked, "Were you just going to sit here and wait today?"

His arm brushed hers and neither of them moved away. "I decided not to run errands and catch up on some reading."

He glanced at the papers in her lap. "What are you reading?"

"Midwifery journal pages I printed from the Internet."

His voice was gentle. "You miss it, don't you?"

"More than you'll ever know."

"Then go back. Start your own practice again. Or send your résumé out."

"I'm still sorting out what I really want."

"No, what you're doing is doubting yourself. Tell me again what you feel is the ideal situation for a baby's birth."

She knew in her heart exactly what that would be, and the words came to her lips easily. "For me, the ideal is having family and friends all around to support the mom, to make her comfortable, to sing and laugh and chase away the fear. There would be soft colors and daylight without harsh spotlights, soothing music and a physician to back me up."

"There *are* hospitals that have birthing centers."

"But those centers sometimes still don't have the right atmosphere. Doctors and nurses rush in and out. Family visits are limited. There are hospital beds instead of birthing chairs, scrub outfits and an institutional feel."

"It doesn't have to be that way. Obstetrical and maternity floors are being redesigned. Maybe you need to be involved in doing that. Maybe you need to be involved in setting up more mom-friendly birthing centers. Don't put limits on your skills or your ideas."

His support felt wonderful. She'd never experienced that type of encouragement.

Jared glanced toward the receptionist's desk. "I'm going to see if I can talk with Mom's therapist. I'll be back."

Ten minutes later he was. "The therapist said she'll be at least forty-five minutes. Do you want to take a walk?"

Emily had learned that Jared walked when he was restless. In the evening sometimes, if he wasn't called away to the hospital, he'd go for a power walk that took him miles away.

Now she asked, "Do you mind if we walk to one of my favorite spots? It's not far. We'll be back in plenty of time."

He cocked his head and examined her as if he were trying to decide where she might take them. Then giving a shrug, he agreed. "Let's go."

As they exited the hospital, Emily turned east, a different direction than they'd taken the night after his mother's surgery.

Eventually they headed into an older neighborhood with stucco houses and tiled roofs. A few were in disrepair, others burst with window boxes laden with fall color.

They strolled in silence until they reached a corner church. It was small as churches went, sunshine yellow with three steps leading to the big brown door.

The door opened before they started up the steps.

"Hello, Padre," Emily greeted the priest who had white hair, dark-brown eyes and a kind smile. She introduced Jared and asked, "Is it all right if we go inside?"

"Of course, my child. Take all the time you want." Then he nodded to them, went down the steps and took the path to the rectory next door.

"Do you come here often?" Jared opened the door for her.

"When I want to think. Or if I need to solve a problem.

Sometimes when I leave the hospital after visiting a new mom, I'm just filled with this joy and I come down here to…absorb it."

Jared was looking at her curiously as if he didn't know her as well as he thought he might.

The church was old with lots of dark, warm wood, cream walls and artful stained glass windows. They walked through the small vestibule. There were only about ten pews on either side with small front alcoves on both the left and the right. Tiny candles blinked in red and blue votive cups.

She moved toward the front pew, Jared beside her. Once there, she murmured to him, "I want to light a few candles. I'll be right back."

She was aware of him settling in a pew while she dug out coins, dropped them in the proper slot, then lit candles for her parents and the Wilsons and their stillborn baby. She stood there a few moments, thinking about them.

When she returned to the pew beside Jared, she knew he'd been watching her.

Again in a low voice, she told him, "I interviewed for a nursing position at the hospital before I interviewed with you. I'd just moved to Sagebrush and I wasn't sure which way to go. I saw this church when I'd driven down the street. I spoke with the padre a long time that day, about everything that had happened. There's something freeing in confiding in a total stranger. He didn't give me any answers, but afterward, I felt freer, ready to begin that new life."

Jared looked around as if he were reacquainting himself with everything he saw. "I haven't been in a church for a long while. I remember going with Mom and Wyatt. Before…everything changed."

Bright September light streamed in the stained glass, making rainbows on the pews.

After a pause, Jared went on. "The lie my mom kept altered my world…and Wyatt's. We were both angry. Their divorce confused me into thinking Wyatt didn't want to *be* my father. But years later he told me that wasn't so. It had hurt him too much to stay, knowing he *wasn't* my father. It hurt too much for him to wonder if my mother really loved him."

"Did you ever ask your mother?"

"No. We don't talk about it."

Emily slid her hand over Jared's, knowing advice wasn't what he wanted to hear. All she could do was support him the way he seemed to support her.

All she could do was love him.

The following evening, Emily was in the kitchen preparing chicken quesadillas for supper when Jared came home. Her breath caught when she remembered yesterday afternoon in the church. She'd slept in her own bedroom again last night, asking herself what came next. If he had feelings for her, would he give in to them?

Today, her questions had taken a backseat to helping his mother with her exercises and playing with the girls. Now Gloria was involved in the twins' fantasy play with their Cinderella coach as Emily worked in the kitchen, wondering if parents should encourage their daughters to believe in fairy tales! All of her questions about her relationship with Jared clicked through her mind again. Whether she herself believed in fairy tales or not, she knew one-sided love would never work.

As always, at the sight of Jared, her heart did a little dance. But then she noticed he wasn't alone. After a second glance at the pretty, young face, she realized who was standing in the kitchen with him. It was Patti and she held her baby in her arms!

"Patti came to the office looking for you," Jared explained.

"Hi," Patti said, crossing to Emily, her smile wide. "I hope you don't mind me tracking you down. Dr. Madison said you were taking care of his daughters. I told him I just wanted to thank you. I don't know what would have happened that day if you hadn't been there."

"I guess you found me through the article in the newspaper," Emily deduced.

"Yes, I did. I thought about sending you a note, but that seemed so inadequate. I wanted to thank you in person by showing you my beautiful baby."

Emily looked down at the infant, so incredibly perfect. She had her mother's features—the tilted-up nose, the high cheekbones, the small chin. "No thanks necessary," she murmured.

"You could have just walked away. You didn't have to get involved. I can't tell you how much it meant to me that you did. I was feeling so alone. The baby's dad didn't want to be a father, so he left a few months ago. My mother and I weren't talking. She was angry with me for getting pregnant. But after you delivered Sandy and I was checked out at the hospital, I called her. We hadn't talked in months, but she came to see me and insisted I go home with her. She and Dad are going to help me with Sandy."

Emily was happy for Patti, that her baby had united her with her parents. "That's wonderful! It's important to have support bringing up a baby. Grandparents are a real gift in so many ways." Emily glanced at Jared, but she couldn't read his expression.

"Would you like to hold her?" Patti asked, bringing Emily's attention back to the baby. "You were the first one who ever held her."

Emily took the baby from Patti's arms, remembering that day with Jared in the nursery.

"You're a natural," Patti joked. "Do you have kids of your own?"

"Not yet," Emily replied. "Maybe someday I'll be blessed to have one of my own."

After a few minutes, Patti scooped Sandy back into her arms. "I don't want to intrude any more on your time."

Jared capped the girl's shoulder. "You're not. In fact, if you'd like to stay for supper, I'm sure we have enough." His gaze checked with Emily.

"Absolutely."

"Oh, I can't," Patti responded. "Mom is expecting me home for dinner, but…" She looked at Emily. "Maybe sometime we could have lunch?"

"I'd like that." Emily went to the counter, wrote her numbers on a slip of paper and handed them to Patti. "My cell phone number and my home number."

"Oh, I thought you were living here."

"I am until Jared's mom gets back on her feet. I share a house in Sagebrush with a friend. You can always reach me on my cell."

"Dr. Madison said you don't work at his practice any longer."

"No, I don't. I was going to work on my résumé tonight."

"But if you were a midwife, why aren't you doing that again?"

"You read the article in the paper," Emily said calmly.

"Delivering a baby that was stillborn must have been absolutely the worst thing in the world. But the paper said you didn't do anything wrong."

"I don't know why the baby was stillborn. What happened still haunts me."

"Seems to me, the best way to make up for it if you feel you have to, is to be delivering lots more healthy babies."

"That's another way of looking at it," Emily agreed, maybe seeing the situation differently for the first time since it had happened.

"I've got to be going," Patti decided. "But I will call you as soon as I get some decent sleep and Sandy gets on a real schedule."

"I'll look forward to hearing from you."

After Patti left, Jared remarked, "I hope I did the right thing by bringing her here. She really did want to thank you in person."

"I'm glad you brought her here."

"She might be right about delivering more babies."

"She's still young…naive."

"That doesn't mean she isn't right."

Emily considered Patti's visit and what Jared had said. "I don't know. Now everyone in Lubbock and the area knows what happened to me. What doctor would back me up?"

"I would."

She studied him for a long moment. "You wouldn't mind being associated with a midwife?"

"We'd have to iron out the conditions and circumstances, how we'd work together. But I think women like Patti need women like you. It's something to think about."

Yes, it was something to think about.

"All day *I've* been thinking that you and I should have a real date," he said, surprising her.

"A *real* date?"

"If you want to. I can make sure there's someone to cover for me tomorrow night."

Did this mean Jared was ready to acknowledge their relationship? Did this mean he might consider a future?

"What about your mom and the girls?"

"I'll see if Chloie can stay with them."

Emily hesitated, only because she wanted to go out with him so much, only because she wanted a future with him more than she'd wanted anything in a very long time.

"Don't feel pressured to say yes. I understand if you'd rather not."

Because he couldn't give her more than one special night? Because he couldn't give her more than terrific sex?

She was going to jump without a parachute. "I want to go out with you, Jared. I want to very much." She thought he might hug her then, maybe even kiss her.

He glanced toward the hall and the bedrooms from where children's laughter floated to them. Instead of doing either, he smiled at her, a very real smile. Emily felt as if he *had* hugged and kissed her.

She couldn't wait for tomorrow night.

Chapter Twelve

Emily stood on the cobblestones at the winery's bed-and-breakfast wondering if she was going to spend the evening alone!

Jared had called to say he'd be late. He told her he would meet her at the bed-and-breakfast's restaurant where he'd made reservations.

She was tempted to stroll down the lane to the wine-tasting room in the rustic, red-tiled building. Her high heels might tilt a bit on the stones—

A car rumbled down the lane, a little faster than it should have been going. Emily smiled. It was Jared.

She maneuvered her way to the parking lot in her high heels. She'd wanted to look nice tonight. She'd worn a mint-colored, silky, fitted blouse with buttons down the front and slacks. Her hair curled free with a copper barrette at her temple.

When Jared climbed out of the car, he just stared at her for a few seconds, a half smile on his lips. Then it faded and she didn't know why.

He was wearing scrubs. "I wanted to get here as soon as I could so you didn't have to wait."

"Were you afraid I wouldn't wait?"

"That was always a possibility."

She saw worry in his eyes and maybe doubts, doubts about his career. "I understand your profession, Jared."

He seemed to relax a bit. "It's your profession, too. Have you given more thought to when you're going to return to it?"

"Are you tired of having me around?"

He slid his hand into her hair and caressed her cheek with his thumb. "No, I'm not tired of having you around. But I think you need to find your niche again."

She had been considering her options, but she was afraid of what would happen when she made inquiries. Besides that, she didn't want to think about it tonight. "I think that subject is way too serious. We're at this beautiful winery and we ought to take advantage of it. Just look at that sunset."

The sky was painted with purple and pink streaks.

"I made reservations for dinner, but I also reserved a room," Jared said, watching her expression. "I'd like to go up and get a shower before we eat. Do you mind?"

"Did you reserve the room just to get a shower?" She was half-teasing, half-serious.

"No. I thought we could have some quiet alone time there away from the world. If you just want to have dinner, that's fine. I'm not pressuring you into anything." He dropped his hand from her cheek as if he had doubts about what she wanted.

"I love the idea of a place where we could have quiet

time without being interrupted. Let's go up and you can get your shower."

"Did I tell you how beautiful you look tonight?"

His words warmed her all over. "No, you didn't. Thank you."

Taking her chin in hand, he gave her a quick kiss, then he returned to the car for his clothes.

The hostess checked them in and changed their dinner reservation to a later hour. They climbed the beautifully polished wood steps, passing photographs on the wall of Buddy Holly, Waylon Jennings and Mac Davis—three musical native sons.

At the landing, they turned right and went to room 2. "I had her describe the rooms to me and I liked the sound of this one."

Emily didn't know what to expect when Jared opened the door. The decor of the bed-and-breakfast seemed to be Western and comfortable.

As Emily stepped into the room, she smiled. This room had a Victorian bent with a huge canopy bed, a small mahogany dresser that looked like an antique, along with a washstand with decorative pitcher and bowl. The windows looked out over the vineyard.

Jared hung his clothes in the closet and dumped his shoes onto the floor. Then he snatched two fluffy white robes from inside and gave one to Emily. "You might want to use it later," he said with a wink.

Jared was usually in busy mode, either busy taking care of his daughters or busy with his career. Now she was seeing the relaxed side of him and she liked it…a lot.

"I won't be long," he said. He pointed to the binder on the dresser. "That's probably a menu if you want to look it over."

Then he disappeared into the bathroom.

She could look over the menu, or—

She heard water begin to run and then the swish of a shower curtain. Suddenly she felt impossibly reckless. She kicked off her high heels and disrobed in a matter of seconds. Then she tiptoed into the bathroom. The ceramic tile was cool under her feet. There was a bathtub in the corner with a shower curtain tucked inside it.

She went to that corner and slid open the curtain a few inches. "Would you like company?"

At the sound of her voice, Jared froze. He was facing the other way and she stared at his wonderfully male body. When he turned around, he saw she was naked, too. His green eyes went darker, and the nerve along his jaw jumped.

"If you'd rather shower alone, I can just get dressed again," she murmured, now unsure.

"You *are* a constant surprise. And that's a compliment."

"I've never done anything this bold," she confided, a bit shyly. She didn't want him to think she ran around jumping into men's showers.

He took the few steps toward her and held out his hands. She took them and climbed over the bathtub rim. They stood that way, face-to-face, holding hands, the water running behind Jared. "Aren't you afraid you'll mess up your makeup? Your hair?"

"I'm only wearing lipstick and a little mascara, and as far as my hair goes, that's why God made hair dryers."

He laughed, a hearty laugh, and wrapped his arms around her. "I knew there was a reason I liked you."

Pushing away slightly, she looked up at him. Teasing sparks lit his eyes. But the longer they stood there, aware of their naked bodies pressed together, aware of their hearts beating in unison, the sparks lit into a fire of hungry desire. She anticipated his kiss and she longed for it.

Instead of kissing her, he reached to the side of the tub and picked up a bar of soap. "I think this could be a lot of fun. Do you want to start, or should I?"

Well, she'd been bold so far. Might as well keep going. Taking the soap from him, she hoped she didn't lose her nerve.

She held her hands out to the water, made a lather, and then began with Jared's chest. He closed his eyes and she hoped that meant he was enjoying her soapy play. *She* certainly was. This was a different kind of making love—a deliberate, pleasure-filled, all-the-time-in-the-world experience.

After she washed his chest, she moved to his arms. Then she asked him to turn around and he raised an eyebrow in surprise.

He rinsed a little, letting water sluice down his back. She took advantage of the wetness, increasing the amount of soap bubbles, letting her fingers slide up and down his neck, over his biceps, around his shoulder blades. Steam filled the room, along with the scent of the soap. The only sound was the splash of the water against the floor of the tub.

Jared stepped back a little, away from the water. She slid her hands down his spine and over his buttocks. His groan was deep.

She was suddenly filled with the desire to make him want her as he'd never wanted her before. She wanted him to desire her so much that he'd never let her leave. She pressed her breasts against his back, her thighs against his, as she wrapped her arms around him and took him into her soapy hands. He sucked in a breath and let her stroke him until he was hot and hard and huge. Before she knew what was happening, he turned and lifted her until her legs went around him.

"Have you ever had sex in a shower before?" His voice was raspy.

"No, have you?"

"No. I guess this will be the first time for both of us."

He walked her to the wall until her back was against it. Then he let her slip down just a little…just enough, and he pressed inside her. He thrust and thrust and thrust again.

Emily came, all of a sudden, all at once, with a blinding ferocity that made every fiber of her body tremble.

Her arms wrapped around his neck and she held on as she cried, "Jared! You make me feel so wonderful."

Her words seemed to tip him over the edge, too, and he shuddered into her, groaning, kissing her as if neither of them ever had to breathe again.

Eventually, he loosened his grip and she let her legs drop, though she wasn't sure she could stand up. He took her face between his hands, gazed at her long and hard and then kissed her again. It was as if he couldn't believe what they'd shared. She couldn't, either.

He called it sex, but she knew they'd had much more than sex. They'd made love.

Jared stepped out of the tub first, found her robe and wrapped her in it. After he lifted her out, he toweled off and wrapped her in his arms again. "Do you want to dress for dinner or call room service?"

"Does that mean we can have supper in bed?" she teased.

"Supper and anything else you want in bed."

"That sounds perfect."

And it would be perfect for tonight. Tomorrow…

Wrapped in Jared's arms, knowing he was going to kiss her again, she hoped tomorrow would take care of itself. She was just going to enjoy tonight.

"Come here, Emily."

The following week Gloria was sitting on the sofa, a photograph album spread over her lap, when Emily returned from the park with Amy and Courtney. Jared's mother was recuperating well, getting stronger each day. She was using a cane now and had it tilted beside her against the sofa.

"What are you looking at?" Emily asked as the twins ran toward their grandmother, gave her a hug and snuggled in, one on each side of her.

"That's Daddy!" Amy proclaimed, pointing to one of the pictures.

Gloria ran her hand over Amy's sun-warmed hair. "It sure is. And I have more pictures when he was much younger. Are you interested?" Gloria asked Emily with a grin.

She definitely was. She felt she and Jared were becoming closer. Since their sojourn at the bed-and-breakfast, she'd joined him every night in his room after everyone else had fallen asleep. He rose early in the morning, so she had plenty of time to go back to her room and get dressed, ready for the day before the twins and Gloria needed her. Whenever she and Jared were alone, they made love. At least that's what it felt like to her. He was so passionate, so tender…

Yet she sensed he didn't want to talk about the future. She sensed that he thought of what they were doing as good sex. It was, but it was so much more. At least she hoped she wasn't deluding herself about that.

Crossing to the sofa, lifting Courtney onto her lap,

Emily watched Gloria pull another photo album from under the first. She positioned it on top and opened it. These photographs were older and were a picturesque time machine back to Jared's childhood.

"He was seven here," Gloria explained, her voice catching a bit. "He was in second grade and all dressed up for the Christmas recital. That was his first suit."

The photo was of Jared standing with a few other children in front of a stage decorated for the holidays.

Gloria's fingers moved from one picture to another. They were fascinating to Emily. She noticed every detail of how Jared had changed through the years.

Finally Gloria's fingers stopped on a studio photograph. This time her thumb gently moved over the figure of the man in the photo. "Wyatt was a wonderful father."

"We were a happy family until I found out what you did." Jared was standing at the edge of the great room. Neither Emily nor Gloria had heard him come in.

Gloria looked up at her son with regret-filled eyes. "I wish I had told Wyatt the truth. I never wanted to hurt either of you."

Jared came over to his daughters, gave both of them a hug and a kiss. After another glance at the album, he said, "There's no point looking at the old photos. The past is in the past."

"I only wish that were true," Gloria said sadly. Then turning to the twins, she suggested, "Why don't you each pick one of your favorite books and we'll read it in my room?"

"Can I make your chair go up and down?" Amy asked.

Gloria laughed. "Before I'm in it."

The girls made a beeline for their bookshelf.

"Do you need help?" Emily asked, knowing Gloria sometimes had problems rising to her feet.

"No. I'm fine, dear." Using her cane, Gloria pushed

herself to her feet. After a last look at her son, she followed her granddaughters to their room.

"You say the past is in the past, but you don't mean it," Emily offered softly after Gloria had left.

Jared lowered himself to the sofa beside her and remained silent.

"Why can't you forgive her?"

He cut Emily a quick glance, then stared into the kitchen. "She deceived me for ten years. Ten years, Emily. I lost the dad I'd respected and admired and loved."

"She didn't want to hurt you, can't you understand that?"

"She knew the truth would come out eventually. She knew I was attached to Wyatt in every way a dad and son bond."

"Exactly. Can't you see why she hoped she could keep the secret forever?"

"That was a fantasy."

"Maybe. Or maybe she thought if the truth came out when you were older, you might understand."

"I can't believe you're defending her!"

"I'm looking at the situation as if I were a mother and wife in the same position she was."

"You wouldn't have kept the truth from your husband. Or would you have?"

From the intensity in his gaze, Emily knew the answer to that question was very important to him. "No. I wouldn't have kept that secret from the man I loved." Would he believe her when she *had* kept her midwifery career from him?

Jared searched her face. After a few heartbeats, he determined, "There's no point discussing this. What happened happened. We all dealt with it the best way we could."

But Emily suspected how much Gloria hurt from the

emotional distance between her and Jared for so many years. "She's your mom, Jared. If you could forgive her, you'd both be so much happier. I'd give anything to talk to my mother again...to hug her. You still have that chance."

When he turned to look at Emily this time, she saw clearly that he wanted her to drop the subject.

After long moments of silence, he covered her hand with his. "How would you like to go out for supper instead of making it? The girls love the cheese fries at Joe's Burger Joint."

Emily knew she couldn't fix Jared's past. She could only concentrate on their future.

"Dr. Madison. *You* are recommending cheese fries?" she joked, letting the past float away...for now.

"Not exactly. But everyone deserves a treat once in a while." He leaned toward her and gave her a long, sensual kiss. "I can't wait until later," he muttered against her lips.

She couldn't, either. She just wished later would bring words of love. She just wished later would bring the promise of a future.

The following day, Gloria carried a plate of tuna salad and carrot sticks to the table as Emily sliced a loaf of bakery bread. The twins were already at their places drinking glasses of milk.

"In another week or so," Gloria said, "I'll be able to do all of this myself. Have you thought about what *you're* going to do?"

Emily had made up her mind. "I'd like to become a midwife again. When I delivered Patti's baby, even though conditions were less than ideal, all the excitement and sense of accomplishment came rushing back. I'm just not sure in what capacity I want to do it."

"You mean home births or hospital births?"

"Yes. I was thinking of submitting a proposal to Lubbock General, maybe initiating a midwife program there."

"Have you talked this over with Jared?"

"I'm still ironing out details in my mind. I think I'd like to write up a proposal, then run it by him."

"Because you're an independent woman of the new millennium," Gloria teased.

Emily laughed. "I guess so."

Emily's cell phone began playing a tune inside her purse. She'd slung it onto the counter when she returned from picking up Gloria from her physical therapy appointment. Now she unzipped the shoulder bag and grabbed her phone, hoping to see Jared's number. He often called just to check up on how his mother and the twins were doing. She was surprised to see *Richard's* phone number.

"Go ahead and eat," she told Gloria and the girls as she walked into the great room and opened her phone, greeting her ex-husband as cordially as she could.

"Can you talk?" he asked.

"Yes," she answered hesitantly.

"I'm in Lubbock and I need to see you. Can you meet me somewhere?"

"You're in Lubbock?"

"I had business. Our radio station is expanding and we're thinking about buying out a broadcasting station here. This trip was a chance to kill both birds with one stone."

"Can't you just tell me what you need on the phone?"

"No. There are a couple of things I need to discuss with you and I'd rather do it in person. Can you get away?"

"Where?"

"There's a restaurant downtown called Charlie's Chuck-wagon. Do you know it?"

She and Tessa and Francesca had enjoyed dinner there a few times. They liked the rustic cowboy atmosphere. "I know it."

"Can you be there in an hour? I'll even buy you lunch. I can put it on my expense account."

Emily's mind was clicking fast. She didn't want to meet her ex-husband. She had the feeling he wanted to talk about finances again. He always did. But if she didn't meet with him, she'd be postponing the inevitable. "Hold on a minute, Richard. I have to check something."

Walking back into the kitchen, she asked Gloria, "Do you think you'd be all right here with Courtney and Amy for about an hour, maybe an hour and a half? I can take my cell phone and if you need me, I can be back here in ten minutes. But if you're not comfortable with being alone with the girls, just say so and I'll postpone this."

Gloria didn't hesitate. "I'll be fine, Emily. We'll read books, do some coloring. You go ahead and meet whoever it is you have to meet."

Emily returned to the great room and the phone. "Instead of Charlie's, can you meet me at the Blue Bonnet Café on Eighty-second Street?"

"That's not anywhere near the hotel or radio station," he grumbled.

"I have responsibilities, Richard. I can't be gone long or go far away."

"All right. In an hour at the Blue Bonnet Café. At least I don't have to travel the whole way to Sagebrush. That's not anywhere near the Family Tree Health Center. Aren't you still working there?"

"No, I'm not. I'm doing something else temporarily."

"Are you telling me you don't have a permanent job?"

From the sound of Richard's voice, this was definitely about finances.

"We'll talk when I see you." Emily closed her phone, went back to the kitchen and dropped it into her purse.

"A problem?" Gloria asked.

Although Emily would like to confide in Jared's mother, she didn't want to pull her into her personal baggage. This was something she had to take care of. Since she didn't know what Richard wanted, there was nothing to confide.

"No, no problem." She took her place at the table and asked Amy and Courtney, "How's the tuna fish?" They both grinned and bobbed their heads up and down.

Emily wished with all of her heart that these two little girls were hers...that Jared's mother was really family.

But she knew too well that wishes often didn't come true. She just hoped Richard didn't have a land mine to drop on her road to happiness.

She'd find out in an hour.

Chapter Thirteen

Jared knew Emily would soon be leaving, and he didn't know what to do about it.

He'd finished with his scheduled delivery earlier than planned, and decided to come home to surprise Emily and the girls. He missed Emily when he was away from her. He found her irresistible. And the chemistry he had with her was different than any he'd experienced in his life so far.

Did he just want to continue their affair? Meet her at her house? Snatch time away at a B and B? Although when he was with her he felt happier than he'd been in years, at other times he was filled with conflict and turmoil. He couldn't help remembering how his mother had deceived his father. He couldn't help reliving how Valerie had resented his profession—the arguments over the late night calls, social plans that crumbled because he'd left for the hospital. Although they'd gotten a divorce, he'd thought they'd kept some measure of a relationship because of their daughters. Yet she hadn't trusted him. She'd gone away and died…alone.

As Jared crossed the kitchen he expected to hear Emily's voice, along with Amy's and Courtney's. Instead, however, he found his mother sitting on the sofa with a coloring book on her lap. Amy and Courtney were kneeling at the coffee table, drawing with crayons.

Maybe Emily was straightening up the twins' room.

"Daddy, you're home," Courtney cried, running to him and tugging on his arm. "See the picture I drawed of Grandma."

Amy grinned at him and came to him, reaching up for a hug. He lifted first one daughter to the ceiling, making her giggle, then the other.

When he turned to his mother, she was smiling at him.

"What?" he asked.

"You're a good dad," she said simply.

The compliment took him off guard. They rarely stepped into personal conversational territory. They seemed to be doing that more. "I try. There just aren't enough hours in a day."

"As long as you give them attention and affection when you *are* with them, that's what is important."

Was that true? Emily had once said something similar. He imagined all single parents felt guilty for the balancing act they had to do between work and their personal lives.

Speaking of his personal life… "Is Emily in the twins' room?"

"No, she's not." His mother checked her watch. "She left about half an hour ago. She had an errand to run."

"She left you alone with Amy and Courtney?"

His mother shrugged. "Look at me, Jared. Yes, I'm using a cane. But I'm almost my old self."

He was disappointed Emily would do this. Had he been so blinded by the chemistry he hadn't seen the side of her that would let responsibility slide? "If you had fallen, or something had happened to one of the twins—"

"Jared," his mother cut in. "She said she'd only be gone an hour."

"What was so important she couldn't wait until I got home?"

He thought about how Emily handled her patients, how she conducted the rest of her life. This really seemed to be a departure.

"She received a call and asked if I would mind if she went out for a little while. I said that was fine."

"A call about a job maybe?" he wondered.

Amy plucked at his shirtsleeve. "She talked to Richard." His daughter looked totally proud of herself that she could supply an answer for him.

But the information made Jared's blood run cold. Richard. Her ex-husband. Why would she be meeting him? Why would Richard be in Lubbock? Why wasn't a phone call good enough if they had something to discuss?

Could her ex-husband realize how much he'd given up in letting her leave? Emily was an intelligent, beautiful, sensual woman. Why would *any* man let her go? If this meeting wasn't a secret, then why not tell his mother about it? Why not tell *him?* Her husband lived in Corpus Christi. It couldn't be spur-of-the-moment. Could it?

Just what did this meeting *mean?*

Emily took a sip of her coffee then returned her gaze to her ex-husband and asked bluntly, "So why did we have to meet face-to-face?"

He'd spent the last fifteen minutes explaining how his radio station was expanding…how Lubbock wasn't the only addition his company wanted to make to their empire. But she'd had enough of his business talk. She needed to get back to Gloria and the twins.

"I'm in a bind."

"A financial bind?" she clarified.

"Yes." His cheeks reddened a little.

She'd always thought Richard handsome. He was five-ten, with light brown hair kept neatly cropped and brown eyes that once had sparkled with interest in her. But now she knew she meant nothing to him except a means to an end. Maybe that's all she'd ever been. He'd looked at his life, decided he needed a wife just as he'd needed a new car or a house in a more prestigious neighborhood. Maybe she had been a rung on a ladder.

"Selling the painting wasn't enough?"

"Not nearly," he admitted. "We were paying interest-only on our mortgage and with property values going down, I can't sell for a profit."

He'd loved their house. More than she had. When he'd asked her for a divorce, she'd moved out and found an apartment. He'd stayed. In the divorce proceedings, she'd discovered they'd had almost no equity in the house. *She* certainly hadn't been able to handle the mortgage payments. Since he'd raided his pension to cover her legal bills, she'd thought it only fair he keep the house.

"What else have you bought?" she asked, knowing he'd been able to cover the mortgage payments quite comfortably before.

He averted his gaze from hers, concentrated on the sandwich in front of him, popped a few chips into his mouth. He shrugged. "I bought a Corvette after you left."

"A Corvette?"

"I'd always wanted one. With you gone, it was a chick magnet."

He'd gone into debt over a chick magnet. "Anything else?"

"This is not about what I bought or didn't buy," he answered angrily. "I helped you when you were in a tough spot. Now I need you to help me."

The guilt card. He'd always played it to his advantage and it had always worked. "I could possibly send you fifty dollars more a month. But I don't know what's going to happen. I'm thinking about becoming a midwife again."

"You *are* kidding."

"No. Why shouldn't I?" Her chin went up and she knew she sounded defensive but couldn't help it.

"Look what happened the last time! Who's going to bail you out now if you get into trouble again?"

Get into trouble again? That's how he saw a child dying on her watch? "Apparently, you still don't understand that there was nothing I could do to prevent that stillbirth. It was *not* my fault."

"Yeah, that's what the jury said. But you thought differently, didn't you? You had doubts."

"Maybe I had doubts because you didn't believe in me. Maybe if you had believed in me, I would have believed in myself." She'd never said this to him before and maybe it was time it came out.

"My believing in you, or not believing in you, wouldn't have changed anything. You still would have had legal bills to take care of, and that's what this is about. I need that money back. Now."

"I can't give it to you *now*. Do you still have the boat?"

His brows drew together. "Yes, I have the boat."

"So that means you still have all the marina fees and the

repair bills." She'd never complained about his toys, but she knew what it cost to keep them.

"So?"

"I did help you pay for that boat. Why don't you sell it?"

"Are you kidding? I take clients out on that boat. I bring in advertising dollars with that boat."

She sighed. "Richard, I *will* pay you back in time. But when I left Corpus Christi, I left with nothing. I didn't want anything. I was grateful to you for helping me out, so I thought you deserved it all. And that included the boat."

Maybe he realized she was finally going to stand up for herself. "Fifty dollars a month is all you can manage? Not a lump sum?"

"Fifty dollars a month."

He was quiet for a while. Finally, he sighed. "I suppose I could just take advertisers to my club."

Richard belonged to a private men's club where he exercised and played racquetball. He also played poker on weekends.

"Unless you want to give up that membership fee," she suggested, knowing it was a hefty one.

With a look of reluctant resignation, he took a paper out from inside his jacket and laid it on the table. "I suspected I'd have to do this. Your name's on the boat. Will you sign this so I can sell it?"

She hadn't made nearly as much as he had. But ever since she'd started working, she'd tucked savings away each month—for a baby someday she'd always thought. But then he'd wanted to buy the boat and it had seemed important to him, so she'd given him those savings and he'd put her name on the title.

She suddenly realized she was at peace about her failed marriage. To Richard, everything had always been about status. She'd left him the house, the boat and his standard of living. Yes, she owed him a debt, and she was going to pay that off. She wished she could do that right now so her marriage would really be in the past. But she couldn't. When she wrote out that check every month, that would remind her what values and goals were really important.

Jared had the same values and goals she did. That mattered. Yet in time, if he couldn't commit to her—

In time, she'd feel more and more like a mom to his girls. In time, they'd feel like a family. But would they *be* a family if Jared couldn't promise her forever?

When Emily walked into Jared's house, she took one look at him and could feel tension build. He'd apparently come home early and hadn't been there long. He was still wearing his white shirt and trousers and hadn't changed. He'd taken off his tie, though, and tossed it onto the counter.

As Gloria levered herself up from the sofa, Jared moved to help her. She reminded him, "I can do it," and he moved away again.

"Come on, girls, let's go to your room and dress your Barbies," she suggested.

"Let's play Barbie," Amy agreed, hopped to her feet and scurried toward her room.

Courtney looked over her shoulder at her dad. "Are you going to play?"

He smiled at her. "Maybe later. I want to talk to Emily. Go ahead."

"I'll help Grandma," Courtney decided, went to her grandmother and took her hand as they walked together to the twins' room.

"You came home early," Emily said, not sure how to dive into a conversation about where she'd been.

"It's a good thing I did. You shouldn't have left my mother alone with Amy and Courtney."

"I knew I wouldn't be gone long. But I wouldn't have gone if I didn't think your mother could handle it."

"She's still unsure of her balance. If she had fallen again—"

Although Jared didn't show it often, he cared about his mother more than he wanted to admit.

"I'm sorry. I was only a phone call away. I told her I'd come right back if she needed me."

Silence lengthened between them until he asked, "What was so important?"

Did he think she was going to lie to him? Hadn't he gotten her message?

"I met with Richard. He was just in town for the day and it was the only opportunity he had. But you should have known that, Jared. I tried to call you before I left. Have you checked your messages?"

He looked blank for a moment, then took the phone from the holster on his belt. He looked chagrined after he checked it. "There's a message there. I was attending an induced labor and just had my pager on."

"Did you think I wouldn't tell you about my meeting?" She really wanted to know what was in his head. A feeling of dread was creeping into her heart. If he didn't trust her, what kind of relationship did they have? Did they *have* a relationship? Or was she only involved in an affair? An affair that would go nowhere?

"You didn't tell my mother. Amy overheard you were meeting Richard."

Apparently Gloria hadn't taken notice of the name as Amy had. "Do you know why I didn't tell your mother, Jared?"

He didn't answer, so she went on anyway. "I wanted to tell her. Actually, I wanted to confide in her. I like your mother very much. But I didn't know if I should."

He looked wary now. "Why?"

"Because I didn't know if I should involve her in my life. I'd love to feel as if she were family. But what would you think about that? The truth is, she's not family. The twins aren't family. I'd love to be their mom, but I'm not. And I don't know if I'll ever be because I don't know what I have with you."

He seemed at a loss to respond to *that* statement. Instead of delving deeper into what she'd said, he asked, "So what did your ex-husband want?"

She let him sidetrack her. Maybe he just needed to get his bearings. Maybe what happened today was a good thing because he'd tell her how he felt about her. "Richard is in a financial bind. He's overextended on his credit and behind in his bills. He asked if I could give him a lump sum."

"What did you tell him?"

"I can't give him a lump sum, so I'm going to send him more each month. I suggested he sell his boat. I signed off on it."

"You told me you gave him everything in the divorce because he'd paid your legal bills."

"I did. He had just never taken my name off the painting or the boat."

Jared shook his head. "He took everything and left you with nothing. He didn't support you when you needed it most. So why are you paying him more?"

"Because I don't want to feel obligated. Because I think it's the fair thing to do." The fair thing to do. She was beginning to realize that she had to be fair to herself and Jared and the twins, too. They were all becoming more attached. She would be leaving soon, and Jared still hadn't told her what he felt for her.

She was standing a good five feet from him. The tension had created at least that much distance between them. Her heart pounded as she moved closer to him, knowing she had to ask him some questions of her own.

His answers would determine her decision.

"Why were you so upset this afternoon?" she asked quietly. "Because I left your mother alone with the girls? Or because I had a meeting with my ex-husband and you thought it was some kind of secret rendezvous?"

"I didn't know what it was. I thought maybe you had planned it," he admitted.

"In other words, you didn't trust me."

His response was slow in coming. "You kept something from me before."

His words sent a chill down her spine. "You're right. I did. Because I was afraid for my job…and I didn't want to mess up what was happening between us. But this is different. We've had weeks together now. I've told you everything there was to tell about me. So why would you doubt me?"

He ran his hand over his forehead. "It's not that simple, Emily."

"Oh, I think it is. What do you *feel* for me, Jared? You've never said. Am I just a capable nanny to take care of your kids? A capable nurse to take care of your mother? Am I just a warm body for your bed? What *am* I to you?"

Her marriage to Richard had filled her with self-doubt and eroded her confidence. She'd left Corpus Christi because she hadn't known how to stand up for herself. But now she did, and these questions had to be asked and answered if she and Jared were going to have a future.

"There's chemistry between us," he answered, almost automatically. "We're good together in bed. I never promised more than that, Emily."

His answer filled her with sadness. "No, you didn't promise more than that. But I began to dream anyway. That was my mistake."

Now she knew what she had to do for both their sakes. Her heart hurt so much she could hardly push out the words. Yet she did. "I think the best thing for both of us is for me to pack up my belongings and go. If Chloie can't stand in, or if you can't find someone to stay with your mom and the girls for a little while longer, I'll do it during the day. But when you come home, I'm gone. It hurts too much to be with you, Jared, knowing I love you but that you don't feel more for me than satisfaction for what we have in bed."

She was still hoping he'd tell her then…tell her that he *did* feel more…tell her that he loved her. But he didn't. He remained silent. And that silence told her she couldn't stay.

Before she started crying, she turned away from him and went to her room, feeling as if her heart was breaking in two.

Jared sank down onto the sofa, stunned by how numb he felt. He couldn't seem to put anything in order. His thoughts were jumbled like puzzle pieces strewn across the table. His mother keeping her secret. His marriage to Valerie. His ex-wife's secret. Emily's secret. Emily's ex-husband.

Jared's mother peeked around the corner from the hall. "The twins are listening to their read-alongs," she informed him, then came to sit beside him on the sofa.

She waited a few moments, he guessed, to see if he'd say anything. But he didn't have any words.

"That didn't sound exactly like a fight," she ventured.

"No. It was an end." Although everything else was jumbled, that fact was clear.

"Do you want it to be an end?"

He stared at his mother, seeing the lines on her face that were a testament to what she'd been through. Not only the surgery and recovery, but her life. And even though he'd kept a wall between them all these years, there was tender concern in her eyes now. And he almost couldn't handle that.

"An end with Emily doesn't feel right," he confessed.

His mother clasped his shoulder, her fingers gripping him tight. "I am sorry for not telling Wyatt the truth. I am so sorry that you felt betrayed."

His mother had said these words before, but they hadn't touched him as deeply as they did now. There were tears in her eyes as she went on. "Because I kept a secret, you can't trust anyone. I don't think you ever trusted Valerie."

"She didn't trust me," he countered.

"Think about your marriage, Jared. Did the two of you share your most intimate secrets? Did the two of you share dreams? That's what trust is all about. I was afraid I'd lose everything I loved if I let the truth come out. Emily was afraid she'd lose her job, and maybe you, if she told you about her background. Valerie was afraid if she stayed here and let you see what was happening to her, that was the way you'd remember her. We all have fears. That's why we can't trust. That's why we can't share."

Suddenly Jared felt as if the room were closing in on him. He felt as if his mother's words were wrapping around him and binding him so tight he couldn't breathe.

"What's wrong?" she asked, apparently seeing what he wasn't saying.

Instead of answering, he asked, "Would you truly be all right here with the twins if Emily leaves? Just for a little while?"

"I'll be fine, Jared. I'm stronger than I look." She gave him a small smile.

"I won't be gone long," he muttered again as he rose, snatched his keys from the counter and went outside.

But he didn't use the car keys. Instead, he walked, passing yards where families lived and played. He walked under Texas ash, caught sight of an older man in a yard trimming back betony, got a whiff of mountain sage. His senses seemed to be more alive, colors brighter. Had this been true since Emily had come into his life?

He walked past the park where she'd played with Amy and Courtney, not because she'd had to, but because she'd wanted to. There was a childlike innocence in Emily, in the way she looked at the world without cynicism. He was so drawn to that.

Before he knew it, he was out of the neighborhood, walking into the hospital district. A short time later he stood before the small mission church where Emily had taken him not so long ago.

As he started up the stairs, the padre came out.

"Good evening," the older priest said. "Can I help you?"

"Is it all right if I just go inside for a few minutes?"

The padre gave him a knowing look and nodded. "Of course."

The heavy door creaked as Jared opened it. The coolness of thick walls, the silence of an empty church, the afternoon light streaking rainbows on the floor rushed toward him and seemed to welcome him.

Candles still flickered in the votive cups on either side of the altar. Jared didn't hesitate to walk toward the front and sit in the first pew. There was solace here if he could reach toward it and find it. He'd felt a little of it that day with Emily.

Soul-searching had never been Jared's forte. Maybe if it had been, his life would be at a better place.

What would make his life better? What did he have to do? How could he keep Emily from leaving?

He realized just how much he wanted to keep her from leaving.

He glanced up at the altar, at the lit candles, at the shimmering light on the wall. He remembered everything his mother had said, and for the first time in his life, he tried to put himself in her place. She'd been scared when she'd learned he wasn't Wyatt's son. She'd loved Wyatt and had been afraid she'd lose him. She'd also been afraid Jared would lose the only father he'd ever known. She'd been right. She'd deceived Wyatt for Jared's sake, too. She'd kept the secret for all their sakes.

His thoughts turned to another important woman in his life. Valerie had married him, thinking a doctor's life was something other than what it was. She'd expected more from him, and he hadn't known how to give it. Had he really tried? Or as his mother had suggested, had he kept a wall around himself, using his career so he didn't have to trust? So he didn't have to share? In the end, Valerie had thought she was doing what was best for him and the twins. Love had directed their actions, right or wrong, and *that's* what he should remember.

When he thought about Emily he couldn't imagine his life without her. He didn't *want* to imagine it. She was more than a nanny. More than a nurse. More than a bedmate. He hadn't wanted to admit that to himself. He hadn't wanted to admit he needed her. Would she stay if he asked her? Would she stay if he opened his heart to her? Because he loved Emily Diaz. He'd lacked the courage to open his heart. He'd lacked the courage to be vulnerable. He'd lacked the courage to trust her. He knew now that trust was a decision as much as a feeling…and so was forgiveness.

Rising to his feet, he stepped over to the side altar, took a bill from his wallet and slipped it into the collection holder. Then he took one of the long sticks from its cup and held it to one of the already lit candles. As he touched the fire to a wick, one flamed for his stepdad, one flamed for Valerie. He also lit one for his mom, for his twins and one for Emily and himself.

After he did, he felt a burden lift from his shoulders.

What if Emily had already left?

He'd go after her. He'd convince her he needed her not only for his twins, but for his own sake.

Because he loved her.

Chapter Fourteen

Jared arrived at Emily's house still uncertain about what he was going to say.

When Francesca opened the door to him, he wondered if Emily had even come home. Her car wasn't in the driveway. But it could be in the detached garage. She'd called Chloie and asked her to come stay with the twins and his mother. But then she'd left, and there hadn't been a trace of her anywhere.

Except for the lingering memories of her—stolen kisses while she was cooking, Emily on the floor, coloring with the twins or having a tea party. In his mind's eye he could see her helping his mother, or he could relive their nights in his room.

The thought that he might have lost her panicked him.

Francesca looked surprised to see him. "I thought," she started, then hesitated. "Never mind," she continued with a smile. "I guess you're here to see Emily?"

"Did she come home?"

He didn't want her to think about this house as home. He wanted her to consider *his* house as *her* home.

"She's in the kitchen, making coffee, though I don't know why she wants coffee. She's already wired, upset—"

"I get the picture," he muttered.

Francesca tilted her head and let him inside. But then she asked, "Are you here to make her smile or cry some more?"

He had the distinct feeling that if he didn't give this woman the right answer, she'd push him back outside. "I hope I'm going to make both of us smile."

Francesca closed the door. "I'll be upstairs in my room with the door shut."

Jared strode into the kitchen and found Emily scooping coffee into a filter. Her eyes grew big when she saw him. "What are you doing here?"

He couldn't just blurt out why he was here. He had to work up to it or she'd never believe him. She'd think he just wanted to get her back into bed.

Still, he crossed the kitchen and stood very close to her. So close he could see the tearstains on her cheeks. He ran his thumb over one, feeling his heart lurch. "I never wanted to hurt you."

"That's why you came? To apologize for hurting me?"

She was obviously trying to help him along. He needed the help. "Not just that. After you left I had a talk with my mother. Actually, I guess she had a talk with me. Maybe it was the first time I really listened to her in years. Anyway, I tried to see her point of view and Valerie's point of view and your point of view."

His heart raced as silence settled between them. She finally broke it with "And could you?"

"I closed a hard shell around my heart a long time ago. But you've been cracking it. Today, I think it broke." He didn't mean to be flip, but he was really having trouble with this.

"What happened when it broke?" She looked hopeful now, and he thought that was a good sign.

"You know that church you took me to?"

She nodded, a perplexed look in her eyes.

"I went there. I thought about everything, and I lit some candles—for my stepdad and Valerie, for Mom, and the girls. And us, too."

Emily's lips parted in surprise and he wanted to kiss her so badly. He was almost there. "When I was sitting in the church, I couldn't imagine my life without you. And not because I want you as a mom for the girls, though I do, because you'd be a wonderful mom. But I realized I've never really let anyone into my heart. I've never opened it before. Not like this. I love you, Emily. I really, really do. I think I've loved you for weeks. I just didn't want to admit it."

He opened his arms to her now, and she didn't back away. She came right into them and asked, "You love me?"

"I do. My work is important to me and it takes up a chunk of my time. It's erratic and calls me out of bed at night. But I promise you, if you marry me, I'll consider your needs along with Courtney's and Amy's first. I think I'm going to actively search to bring someone else into our partnership so we all have more leisure time. Can you forgive me for doubting your truthfulness? Can you forgive me for not seeing sooner what was in front of my face?"

Reaching her arms around his neck, she laced her fingers in his hair. "I love you, Jared Madison," she said joyously. "I can forgive you if you promise to keep telling me how you feel."

"I'll do better than that." His lips were very close to hers now. "I'll tell you how much I love you every single day and I'll whisper my dreams to you, too."

"Dreams of our life together?" she asked.

"Dreams for us, the girls and our life until we both have silver hair."

Picking her up so that her mouth was even with his, he sealed his lips to hers. His kiss promised a future and vows that would last forever.

Epilogue

"This is definitely an unconventional honeymoon," Jared said as he smiled at Emily. He was carrying Courtney and she was carrying Amy, as they entered the suite at one of the hotels at Disney World.

"Everything we've done has been a bit unconventional." She returned his smile and followed him into the living room of their suite.

Jared couldn't believe the happiness filling his heart. He and Emily had married in a quiet ceremony with only his mother, cousin, Vince, Tessa and Francesca present. He and Emily had spent the night at the bed-and-breakfast at the winery, and then the following day they'd gotten on a plane to Disney World, Amy, Courtney, his mother and Chloie included.

Both girls squiggled to be let down. They ran through the open door to the adjoining room.

Jared took the opportunity to encircle his new wife's waist and bring her close for a resounding kiss. After they broke apart, he joked, "I guess they want to tell Mom about It's a Small World."

"Or about the Country Bear Jamboree," she teased, holding hands with him as they joined the girls in his mother's room.

Gloria was sitting in an easy chair by the window, reading. At least, she had been reading. Now the girls were chattering away, bubbling over with the sights and sounds and smells of a day in strollers at the amusement park.

His mother stood, still depending on her cane, but much stronger than she'd been a month before. Jared couldn't believe it was already the middle of October. And the upcoming holiday season was going to be like no other he'd ever experienced, with family and friends and a beautiful, caring wife who made each day special.

Emily went over to his mother. "Did you have a good afternoon?"

"It was lovely. I spent some time in the garden. And there are such interesting people to talk to…from all over."

"Are you sure you don't want to go to the park with us tomorrow? If Chloie joins us, we'll have an extra set of hands to push the wheelchair. I think you'd like some of the attractions."

"I'm really just fine right here. This is a wonderful vacation, sitting on the patio in the sun, drinking iced tea, watching all the people. But I'll think about your suggestion. Maybe I'll venture out with you tomorrow."

Jared's relationship with his mother had changed since the day they'd had their talk. The past really had seemed to drop away, and they were building memories for the future. He and his partners had almost settled on another doctor to come into the practice. Emily was going to start advertising her services as a midwife, and he was going to be her backup at the hospital. The hospital was also considering her proposal to start a midwifery program there. Professionally, they were going to be a team. Personally, they were *already* a team.

Suddenly, there was the sound of a card key in the lock and then Chloie burst into his mom's room. "I hope I'm not late," she said. "I know you two want to go out tonight."

"Not at all," Emily assured her. "I'm going to take a shower and change and get a little more dressed up."

As she came toward him, Jared hooked an arm around her waist. "You're perfect the way you are."

She looked down at her shorts and knit top. "I think I can do a little bit better than this. Where did you disappear to this afternoon?" Emily asked Chloie.

Jared thought his cousin actually blushed. She had split off from them, having different interests than the attractions they'd planned to visit with the twins.

"Actually, I spent the afternoon talking to someone."

"Someone?" Jared asked, his radar sensing something.

"I was on the Jungle Cruise and started talking with this science teacher from Galveston."

"Male or female science teacher?" Jared asked.

Emily poked him in the ribs.

Chloie blushed some more. "Male. We spent most of the afternoon talking. We exchanged e-mail addresses and cell-phone numbers, and within the next couple of days when you don't need me, I might meet him for lunch or dinner."

"Is that when I can check him out?" Jared asked, sounding like an older brother.

Chloie winked at him. "I might let you do that."

Satisfied, Jared took Emily's hand and went to their suite to get ready for their evening together.

Emily stood on Main Street at Disney World, her new husband's arms wrapped around her, as they watched the last flicker of lights from the parade fade away. Unconventional though it might be, this was a wonderful honeymoon. They'd had dinner at a delicious restaurant, strolled hand in hand, kissing every once in a while and then found a place here to watch the magic of the light parade.

They were standing across from Cinderella's castle and Emily couldn't help but smile. "We bought the girls Mickey Mouse hats while we were here, but we need to buy you one, too."

He kissed her temple. "What kind of hat do you want to buy for me, or shouldn't I ask?"

"I want to buy one for you that says 'Prince Charming.'"

He nudged her around to face him. "You're serious, aren't you?"

She circled his neck with her arms. "Very. I'm happier now than I've ever been in my whole life. That's because of you."

He was quiet for a moment, glanced at the castle and then back at her. "I never thought I'd deserve someone like you."

He pulled something out of his pocket. "You were looking at these in the souvenir store. So I thought I'd buy one for you."

Jared took her hand and turned it palm up. Then he set a miniature glass slipper in her hand.

Tears came to her eyes at his thoughtfulness. "Oh, Jared! It's beautiful. Thank you."

Wrapping his arms around her again, he said, "You've convinced me to believe in fairy tales. *And* happy endings."

When Jared bent his head and kissed her, Emily kissed him back fervently, remembering the vows they'd taken and the promises they'd made.

He reluctantly pulled away, stole another tender kiss then took her hand. As long as he held on to her, their future would be as bright and shiny as the lights on Cinderella's castle. Her Texas doctor had been Prince Charming in disguise all along. She felt like the luckiest woman in the kingdom.

Jared squeezed her hand then released it to wrap his arm around her. Their honeymoon was just the beginning of the rest of their lives.

* * * * *

Don't miss the next installment in
Karen Rose Smith's
THE BABY EXPERTS *miniseries,*
on sale August 25, 2009,
from Silhouette Special Edition.

In honor of our 60th anniversary,
Harlequin® American Romance® is celebrating
by featuring an all-American male each month,
all year long with
MEN MADE IN AMERICA!
This June, we'll be featuring American men
living in the West.

Here's a sneak preview of
THE CHIEF RANGER by Rebecca Winters.

Chief Ranger Vance Rossiter has to
confront the sister of a man who died
while under Vance's watch...and also
confront his attraction to her.

"Chief Ranger Rossiter?" The sight of the woman who'd stepped inside Vance's office brought him to his feet. "I'm Rachel Darrow. Your secretary said I should come right in."

"Please," he said, walking around his desk to shake her hand. At a glance he estimated she was in her midtwenties. Her feminine curves did wonders for the pale blue T-shirt and jeans she was wearing. "Ranger Jarvis informed me there's a young boy with you."

The unfriendly expression in her beautiful green eyes caught him off guard. "Yes," was her clipped reply. "When we arrived in Yosemite the ranger told me I couldn't go anywhere in the park until I talked to you first."

"That's right."

"Knowing you wanted this meeting to be private, he offered to show my nephew around Headquarters."

So this woman was the victim's sister.... "What's his name?"

"Nicky."

The boy who haunted Vance's dreams now had a name. "How old is he?"

"He turned six three weeks ago. Were you the man in charge when my brother and sister-in-law were killed?"

"Yes. To tell you I'm sorry for what happened couldn't begin to convey my feelings."

The woman's gaze didn't flicker. "I won't even try to describe mine. Just tell me one thing. Was their accident preventable?"

"Yes," he answered without hesitation.

"In other words, the people working under you fell asleep on your watch and two lives were snuffed out as a result."

Hearing it put like that, he had to set the record straight. "My staff had nothing to do with it. I, myself, could have prevented the loss of life."

Ms. Darrow's expression hardened. "So you admit culpability."

"Yes. I take full blame."

A look of pain crossed over her features. "You can just stand there and admit it?" Her cry echoed that of his own tortured soul.

"Yes." He sucked in his breath.

"I work for a cruise line. Aboard ship, it's the captain's responsibility to maintain rigid safety regulations. If a disaster like that had happened while he was in charge he would have been relieved of his command and never given another ship again."

Rachel Darrow couldn't know she was preaching to the converted. "If you've come to the park with the intention of bringing a lawsuit against me for negligence, maybe you should." It would only be what he deserved.

"Maybe I will."

In the next instant, she wheeled around and hurried out of his office. Vance could have gone after her, but it would cause a scene, something he was loath to do for a variety of reasons. In the first place, he needed to cool down before he approached her again.

The discovery of the Darrows' frozen bodies had affected every ranger in the park. A little boy had been orphaned—a boy whose aunt was all he had left.

* * * * *

Will Rachel allow Vance to explain—
and will she let him into her heart?
Find out in
THE CHIEF RANGER
Available June 2009 from
Harlequin® American Romance®.

Copyright © 2009 by Rebecca Burton

HARLEQUIN
60 YEARS
of pure reading pleasure.

We'll be spotlighting a different series every month throughout 2009 to celebrate our 60th anniversary.

Look for Harlequin®
American Romance® in June!

Join us for a year-long celebration of the rugged American male! From cops to cowboys— Men Made in America has the hero you've been dreaming about!

MEN
Made in America
American ★ Romance

Look for

The Chief Ranger

by Rebecca Winters, on sale in June!

HARLEQUIN Romance

Escape Around the World

Dream destinations, whirlwind weddings!

Honeymoon with the Boss
by
JESSICA HART

Top tycoon Tom Maddison is used to calling the shots—until his convenient marriage falls through. But rather than waste his honeymoon, he'll take his boardroom to the beach and bring his oh-so-sensible secretary Imogen on a tropical business trip! But will Tom finally see the sexy woman that prudent Imogen truly is?

Available in June wherever books are sold.

www.eHarlequin.com   HR175900

New York Times **bestselling author**

SHERRYL WOODS

draws you into a world of friendships,
families and heartfelt emotions in
her brand-new Chesapeake Shores series.

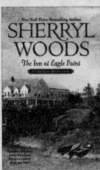  

On sale March 31 *On sale April 28* *On sale May 26*

MIRA®

www.MIRABooks.com

MSWTRI09

**Stay up-to-date
on all your romance
reading news!**

The Inside Romance
newsletter is a **FREE**
quarterly newsletter
highlighting
our upcoming
series releases
and promotions!

Go to
eHarlequin.com/InsideRomance
or e-mail us at
InsideRomance@Harlequin.com
to sign up to receive
your **FREE** newsletter today!

You can also subscribe by writing to us at: HARLEQUIN BOOKS
Attention: Customer Service Department
P.O. Box 9057, Buffalo, NY 14269-9057

Please allow 4-6 weeks for delivery of the first issue by mail.

IRNBPA0109

REQUEST YOUR FREE BOOKS!

2 FREE NOVELS PLUS 2 FREE GIFTS!

SPECIAL EDITION®

Life, Love and Family!

YES! Please send me 2 FREE Silhouette Special Edition® novels and my 2 FREE gifts (gifts are worth about $10). After receiving them, if I don't wish to receive any more books, I can return the shipping statement marked "cancel." If I don't cancel, I will receive 6 brand-new novels every month and be billed just $4.24 per book in the U.S. or $4.99 per book in Canada. That's a savings of at least 15% off the cover price! It's quite a bargain! Shipping and handling is just 50¢ per book.* I understand that accepting the 2 free books and gifts places me under no obligation to buy anything. I can always return a shipment and cancel at any time. Even if I never buy another book from Silhouette, the two free books and gifts are mine to keep forever.

235 SDN EYN4   335 SDN EYPG

Name _____ (PLEASE PRINT)

Address _____ Apt. #

City _____ State/Prov. _____ Zip/Postal Code

Signature (if under 18, a parent or guardian must sign)

Mail to the **Silhouette Reader Service:**
IN U.S.A.: P.O. Box 1867, Buffalo, NY 14240-1867
IN CANADA: P.O. Box 609, Fort Erie, Ontario L2A 5X3

Not valid to current subscribers of Silhouette Special Edition books.

Want to try two free books from another line?
Call 1-800-873-8635 or visit www.morefreebooks.com.

* Terms and prices subject to change without notice. Prices do not include applicable taxes. Sales tax applicable in N.Y. Canadian residents will be charged applicable provincial taxes and GST. Offer not valid in Quebec. This offer is limited to one order per household. All orders subject to approval. Credit or debit balances in a customer's account(s) may be offset by any other outstanding balance owed by or to the customer. Please allow 4 to 6 weeks for delivery. Offer available while quantities last.

Your Privacy: Silhouette is committed to protecting your privacy. Our Privacy Policy is available online at www.eHarlequin.com or upon request from the Reader Service. From time to time we make our lists of customers available to reputable third parties who may have a product or service of interest to you. If you would prefer we not share your name and address, please check here. ☐

SSE09R